VIPER M

Nick Ryan

A World War 3 Technothriller Action Event

Copyright © 2021 Nicholas Ryan

The rights of Nicholas Ryan to be identified as the author of this work have been asserted by him in accordance with the copyright, Designs and Patents Act 1988.

This is a work of fiction. Names, characters, places, and incidents either are the product of the author's imagination or are used fictitiously. Any resemblance to actual persons, living or dead, events, or locales is entirely coincidental.

All rights reserved. No part of this publication may be reproduced, stored in or introduced into a retrieval system, or transmitted, in any form, or by any other means (electronic, mechanical, photocopying, recording or otherwise) without the prior written permission of the author. Any person who does any unauthorized act in relation to this publication may be liable to criminal prosecution and civil claims for damages.

Dedication:

This book is dedicated to my fiancé and my inspiration – Ebony.

-Nick.

About the Series:

The WW3 novels are a chillingly authentic collection of action-packed combat thrillers that envision a modern war where the world's superpowers battle on land, air and sea using today's military hardware.

Each title is a 50,000-word stand-alone adventure that forms part of an ever-expanding series, with several new titles published every year.

Facebook: https://www.facebook.com/NickRyanWW3
Website: https://www.worldwar3timeline.com

Other titles in the collection:
- 'Charge to Battle'
- 'Enemy in Sight'
- 'Viper Mission'

The Fight For Ukraine

When World War III in Europe broke out across the Baltic States, Ukraine instinctively braced for an imminent Russian attack.

The Ukraine government made frantic preparations, massing troops, armor and fighter aircraft along its eastern border, anticipating the inevitable spark that would ignite a powder keg of savage fighting.

Lithuania, Estonia and Latvia fell to the invading enemy. The Russian spearhead steamrolled into Poland, driving towards Warsaw.

Then – two weeks after the first eruption of brutal fighting – Russian tanks came pouring across the Ukrainian border.

War came to Ukraine behind a wall of heavy artillery, a veil of choking smoke and a tidal wave of mechanized infantry. The sky filled with Russian fighter-bombers and the waters off the country's coastline turned red with blood.

The Government in Kiev held its breath. Russia attacked on multiple fronts, surging across the eastern border, landing special forces troops behind the lines, and then opening a second front in the northern region of the country with orders to close on the capital and seize the city.

The Ukraine government issued an urgent plea to western nations for support but it was several days before the first US F-16 Vipers arrived in-country and were ready to commence operations.

Meanwhile the devastation and the death toll rose. On every front the Ukraine Army was being driven back by an overwhelming enemy. After just a few days, the capital city was reduced to rubble, and the Ukraine Air Force had been decimated. Russia dominated the skies over the northern and eastern fronts, and the Ukraine troops were driven back in disarray.

The ground war became a bitter bloody struggle, with the Russians grinding forward relentlessly and the Ukrainians fighting to contest every inch of ground. The skies became filled with trails of missile smoke and sleek twisting fighters gripped in a supersonic duel to the death.

Outnumbered and exhausted, the Allied pilots flew endless missions to stall the speed of the Russian ground attacks and to fight for air superiority. Day after day the fighter pilots took to the sky to dice with death.

For the handful of heroic American F-16 Viper pilots flying round-the-clock missions from their makeshift air base in the west of the country, losses were inevitable. Despite the dangers they flew on, rising into the sky each day to meet every Russian challenge.

They were bleak days of ferocious fighting where no quarter was asked for or given. They were nights of harrowing bombing missions and crushing exhaustion.

Yet the Americans and their Ukraine allies fought on.

In the war-torn skies, young American pilots learned the stark cruelty of combat, and paid the ultimate price for freedom.

LUTSK AIR BASE
WESTERN UKRAINE

Chapter 1:

"This isn't what I signed on for," declared Steve 'Lone Wolf' McQuade, and screwed up his face into a sneer of contempt before he went on. "Why the hell are we fighting their war for them anyhow?" He slammed the door of the van shut and stepped out onto the flightline; his eyes adjusting to the Ukraine morning light.

"This is *exactly* what you signed on for." Flight leader Ron 'Magic' Hernandez lifted his eyes to the cloudless sky and blinked several times.

"No way, man. I enlisted to protect America from its enemies. Take a look around. This sure as hell ain't Kansas." He began striding towards the hangars.

"You are protecting America from its enemies," Hernandez spoke without any real conviction. He cast a glance sideways at his wingman for the mission and shook his head.

"It's just not right," muttered McQuade. "I don't want to die in some god-forsaken European hell hole. I don't mind fighting. I'm not afraid to go into battle – but I don't even know what I'm supposed to be fighting for."

"America is at war with Russia," said Hernandez testily. "Right now, that war is happening here in Ukraine." The verge of the runway at Lutsk Air Force Base was cracked and overgrown with weeds. A week before the base had been inactive. Now it was home to a squadron of American F-16C Block 52 Vipers who were flying missions in support of the Ukraine government's efforts to defend its eastern and northern borders against invading Russian columns of tanks and troops.

"I reckon every man should know why he's in a fight," McQuade opined. "Christ, I've never even met a Ukrainian! I wouldn't know one if I bumped into one. I don't even know the damned language. So why the hell should I care whether

Russia invades their country? America is thousands of miles away."

"America stands for freedom," Hernandez said. "If we don't confront countries like China and Russia, who will?"

"Who cares?" McQuade spat back. "Do you think anyone in Ukraine cares about me? Why should I care about them?"

"Innocent people are dying in Russian attacks every day, bucko," an edge came into Hernandez's voice. "They're people just like me and you – people like your mom and dad. They're being bombed out of their homes, their towns are being overrun by Russian soldiers, their lives torn apart. You might not know them but they're innocents. Someone has to fight for them."

They reached the hangar and stepped into gloomy shadow. The two F-16s stood side-by-side, sleek and needle-nosed birds of prey, crouched like impatient animals, eager to be unleashed.

Hung from pylons beneath each fighter's wings were two MK-84 general purpose bombs that weighed two thousand pounds apiece. The MK-84s were the monsters of aerial bombardment, capable of generating craters fifty feet deep with a killing radius close to a thousand feet. The sight of the bombs prompted McQuade to fresh complaint.

"Tell me again why we have to do this old school?"

"Old school?"

"Yeah, low altitude MK-84 dumb bombs like in the days of the God-damned Gulf War."

Thirty years earlier low altitude bombing runs were the accepted mode of attack to strike targets, but since the '90s tactics and weapons had changed dramatically. It was now conventional for American pilots to fly high altitude bombing missions armed with smart bombs.

"Because we got here in a hurry," Hernandez said flatly. In truth, he was none-too-pleased about the mission either, but he kept his opinion to himself. "And we're the only fighter squadron in Ukraine. Until the ammunition catches up with us, we fly with what we have. It may not be pretty, but it's got to be done. The targets can't wait until the logistical support catches up with us, so suck it up and do your job."

The two pilots locked eyes, tension simmering between them. McQuade made to walk towards his fighter, but Hernandez snatched at his arm to hold him back. "I read your record. You're a military brat. You're a selfish son-of-a-bitch who did well at pilot training but was criticized for lacking the ability to work in a team. I hope they beat that hero bullshit out of you at ENJJPT, because we ain't got room for Tom Cruise 'Maverick' games in a war zone. Got it?"

McQuade had attended the USAFA Air Force Academy in Colorado Springs, finishing near the top of his class and then been selected for ENJJPT (Euro-NATO Joint Jet Pilot Training Program) at Sheppard AFB in Wichita Falls, flying with the 80th. His last posting before being flown on a C-17 transport to Spangdahlem Air Base was with the 311th flying out of Holloman AFB in New Mexico. He was well-credentialed and talented, the son of a retired USAF General and former combat pilot. But to Ron Hernandez, McQuade was just another arrogant rookie with an inflated opinion of his own abilities. Hernandez had seen it all before. The cemeteries were filled with hot-shots.

"Got it, read the book, and seen the movie," Steve McQuade's lip curled with scorn. "I spent a week getting mission-ready with the 480th. I've had the same lecture from a dozen instructors. I know the drill."

Hernandez shook his head and let go of McQuade's arm. "Uncle Sam has spent millions of dollars teaching you how to fly and fight a Viper, and in all that time they never once spent a nickel teaching you common sense or humanity. I hope you live long enough to learn the lesson…"

*

McQuade's crew chief was a young airman with a pale complexion and ginger hair. He snapped a salute and the two men shook hands. He took McQuade's data file and placed it in the jet.

"Sir, your Mode Two?"

"One-nine-nine-four."

McQuade climbed up the ladder carrying his flight gear while the crew chief opened a narrow compartment in the nose section of the Viper and programmed the aircraft's squawk. McQuade checked the cockpit switches, set his helmet on the canopy rail and leaned down to insert his DTC into its slot. The cartridge carried the data of the mission profile. In the days before DTC pilots had to hand-program the navigation route, weapons conditioning and release information as well as steerpoint latitude and longitude, elevation and any offset aimpoints.

The digital data transfer completed, McQuade climbed back down the ladder and circled the jet, performing the aircraft preflight. The crew chief handed him a stick of white chalk. McQuade wrote, *'Fuck Russia'* on one of the huge **MK-84** bombs and *'Lone Wolf'* on the other.

Ten minutes before engine start, McQuade pulled on his gloves as the crew chief helped connect his parachute harness. The pilot settled himself in the cockpit. He looked left and saw Hernandez staring back at him. McQuade's crew chief followed him up the ladder and strapped him in. The two men shook hands again.

"Good luck, sir. Kill those Commie fuckers."

McQuade gave the young airman a cocky grin and slid his helmet on. He connected his oxygen hose and microphone, then settled himself deep in the narrow, reclined seat. He could feel the sudden surge of adrenalin beginning to fizz in his blood. His heart rate began to rise. Tiny insects of anxiety and tension crawled beneath his skin. He strapped his checklist and lineup card to his thighs then sucked in a few deep settling breaths. The air was thick with the stench of Avgas.

Finally, McQuade turned on the aircraft battery and motored down the canopy. He checked his watch. In his headset the crew chief's voice crackled suddenly.

"Your intake has been checked and is clear, sir," he said. "And the fireguard is posted and standing by."

"Roger, chief."

McQuade stole a furtive glance out through the bubble canopy. Hernandez sat calmly in his fighter, his expression unreadable behind the oxygen mask and helmet visor.

Both jets started their engines at the prebriefed time.

McQuade switched the aircraft's Jet-fuel starter to Start One. The engine began to spool up. When the RPM counter rose to twenty percent, McQuade slid the throttle into idle and the huge engine screamed to life. The entire airframe began to vibrate. The flightline became a thunder of screaming noise as both pilots completed their checklist items. The crew chiefs dashed forward and removed the chocks from both Vipers wheels. Hernandez's F-16 taxied towards the departure end of the runway. McQuade released the brakes and his fighter began to roll, following. His crew chief offered a final crisp salute. McQuade saluted back, then fell in alternating line behind Hernandez's Viper.

The arming area was at the southern end of the runway. McQuade parked alongside Hernandez's jet and tried to control a sudden spasm of shivering nerves. The arming crews swarmed around both fighter jets to make final inspections of each huge bomb.

The F-16s had the runway to themselves. The sky overhead was a vast blue dome. After several minutes the Vipers finally taxied onto the runway and Hernandez visually gave the 'run-up' signal, twisting his hand with two fingers extended. Seconds later Hernandez released the brakes and commenced his takeoff roll. McQuade saw the Viper's afterburner flare as it ignited, quivering the air into a shimmer of heat haze. McQuade waited twenty seconds and then followed. He pushed up the fighter's throttle to eighty percent RPM and then released the brakes. The force of the Viper's sudden acceleration pressed him into his seat as the jet flashed down the runway and then leaped gamely into the air.

*

The Vipers lifted into the sky and climbed quickly to twenty-five thousand feet. Their mission was a bombing attack against two Russian targets on the outskirts of Kiev. The first objective was a fuel depot located thirty-one miles south of the capital and the second, in the city's eastern suburbs, was a Russian Army military command post. Both F-16s would drop one MK-84 on each target.

McQuade peered through the bubble of his canopy. Up ahead, vast banks of thunderheads were rearing up from a low wall of cumulus nimbus, thrusting into the sky like avalanches of silver and grey and soft blue. Each thunderhead was separated by deep crevasses and the shapes were twisted and tortured into a splendor of majestic towers. Higher up, the sky was a darkening blue, and between the swelling cloud mountains the sunshine spilled down on the two fighters.

Visibility between the clouds was as much as fifty miles; the great dome of the earth below was fringed by a hazed horizon where the land and sky were smudged together by a black scar of smoke.

The jets flew due east at high speed for ten minutes before they reached their refueling point. McQuade detected the tanker on radar, thirty miles off his nose. The aircraft was a KC-135 Stratotanker. McQuade's Viper joined on the KC-135's right wing. Hernandez joined just below the boom. He held a position five hundred feet from contact for a few seconds and then drifted effortlessly forward to hook up to the tanker. McQuade watched on from his cockpit.

"Spartacus One, disconnect," Hernandez came off the boom and swung on to the Stratotanker's left wing.

McQuade cycled his Viper into the pre-contact position.

Air-to-air refueling required patience and composure. McQuade pulled his throttle back and dropped down smoothly behind the tanker, then touched up the power to stall his backward momentum. When he looked up through the top of the clear canopy, he saw the Stratotanker's boom operator positioned in the lower section of the huge aircraft's aft fuselage. McQuade glanced at his HUD to get his bearings. He was cruising at a touch over three hundred knots at an altitude of twenty-four thousand feet. He gave the boomer a thumbs-up signal to let him know he was ready to proceed.

The boom spooled out from the fuselage of the tanker, undulating like the unfolding body of an enormous funnel-headed snake. McQuade gave his throttle a nudge up, flying directly at the boom. Aboard the KC-135 the boomer fiddled with his onboard control stick, steering the winged re-fueling probe to the refueling port located aft of the Viper's canopy on the upper side of the fuselage. As soon as the boomer slotted the probe into port, McQuade's nosewheel steering gauge showed a green 'connect' light. The young pilot was tempted to let out a sigh of relief, but he knew Hernandez would be watching him with a critical eye and McQuade had a point to prove. He kept his gaze fixed on the signal lights located on the underbelly of the KC-135 that activated the moment the refueling probe was in place. The lights were there to help the pilot being refueled maintain good contact and flashed to indicate forward, aft, up and down directions if the aircraft was straying out of position.

When the Viper's fuel tanks were topped off, McQuade thumbed the disconnect button on the side of his control stick and eased his fighter back until he had cleared the boom.

"Spartacus Two, disconnect," McQuade radioed laconically. He swept left, positioning himself outside of Hernandez's F-16 in a loose route position.

Below the Vipers the landscape of rural western Ukraine was a ragged patchwork of greens and dirty dull browns, flat featureless plains and gentle plateaus sprinkled with small villages and dirt roads. It was bleak terrain, fringed by dense expanses of dark green forest spilt by the meandering passage of winding rivers. McQuade wondered for a moment about the people that lived in those small villages and isolated farmhouses. Did they celebrate Christmas? Did they believe in

God? Did they have televisions, or play baseball on weekends? He had no idea.

Hernandez porpoised his jet, signaling McQuade into tactical formation. The young pilot pushed his throttle up to military power and drifted further left until the two Vipers were around ten thousand feet apart with McQuade flying three hundred feet above Hernandez's wing.

With each passing minute the tension increased. The Vipers were less than five minutes from the FEBA (Forward Edge of the Battle Area). As they crossed into eastern Ukraine, where the ground war was raging, McQuade spotted the shaded outline of a wedge-shaped plateau that marked their descent point and the outer edge of hostile territory.

Hernandez's voice crackled in McQuade's headset. "Spartacus Two, go Victor eleven, fence in!"

McQuade switched his VHF radio to channel 11 and made one final check of his aircraft systems as the fighters prepared to flash across the 'fence' into war-torn territory. He adjusted the range of his radar to forty-mile scope and fiddled the search altitude until it read 20,000 feet and above. The rest of the procedures he completed instinctively; activating his electronic countermeasure pod, adjusting the volume on his radar threat warning receiver and arming his chaff and flare systems. His eyes drifted over his fuel indicators and then swept the sky around him warily, looking for the approaching dark dot of a Russian fighter.

As the Vipers approached the gentle rise of the escarpment, Hernandez initiated a combat descent and the two F-16's rolled inverted and plunged towards the earth. McQuade pulled the nose of his fighter down until it was aimed at the ground. The Viper accelerated rapidly, despite the massive burden of the huge bombs its carried. Finally, he rolled upright again and gradually decreased the angle of his descent. Within sixty seconds the fighters had plummeted from twenty-four thousand feet to just five hundred feet above the ground, and had accelerated to almost five hundred knots.

The terrain beyond the nose of McQuade's jet blurred. Dense tracts of dark green forest leaped up from the rim of the horizon and then a moment later had blown by. A winding river snaked beneath his right wing. Open fields of brown dry grass and the peaked rooftops of buildings all disappeared beneath the nose of the jet, distorted by speed. McQuade flew by instinct and let his thoughts drift to the details of the mission.

The pilots had been warned at their pre-flight briefing to expect both targets to be heavily defended by enemy SAM systems. There was intelligence speculation that a Battalion of the lethal SA-21 Growlers were positioned around the outskirts of Kiev, consisting of at least eight launchers with thirty-two missiles and a mobile command post. The system had the ability to track and target up to thirty-six aircraft at a range of one hundred and fifty kilometers. Supplementing the SA-21s was a loose ring of older SA-8 Gecko missile sites to defend against low altitude attacks.

The Vipers flew on towards their IP (Initial Point) which was the last checkpoint before they engaged the fuel depot target. McQuade kept scanning the sky overhead, looking for the telltale sign of an enemy fighter jet. His RWR (Radar Warning Receiver) remained eerily quiet. Hernandez's voice broke through the tense silence.

"Spartacus Two, master arm on."

McQuade dutifully flipped the fighter's master arm switch from 'Simulate' to 'Arm'. A trickle of cold sweat ran down his spine.

The mission IP was a small distinct village that stood out because of its perch atop a gentle rise of land. The two jets flashed over the rooftops of the village and accelerated to five hundred and sixty knots, turning twenty-five degrees to the right to position themselves on the run-in heading to the fuel depot. Around them the terrain became a vast flat plain of gently undulating featureless farmland, split by a ribbon of bleak grey road.

McQuade wriggled in his seat, flexed his fingers, and sucked in a deep breath, preparing himself for the next few minutes of high-stress danger. On his HUD the Viper's distance measuring equipment counted down the range to target.

Suddenly Hernandez's voice, thick with tension, burst across the radio.

"Spartacus One, Mud 8, two-three-zero!"

The fighters had been detected by one of the SA-8 Gecko missile sites posted around the perimeter of the enemy fuel depot.

Now the fighting would begin.

*

The radar warning receiver on the upper left side of McQuade's cockpit lit up to indicate the Russian SAM site's radar had acquired his fighter. The icon on his scope was lit by a green diamond and suddenly the pilot's headset filled with a warbling sound of warning.

McQuade scanned the horizon line. The road from the village ran parallel to his course, past a dense tract of forest off his left wing. Up ahead he could see a sharp turnoff road that led to a clearing within the forest canopy where the enemy fuel dump was concealed. The storage tanks and pipelines were hidden under a vast web of camouflage netting. Tiny dark specks on the road were fuel trucks, lined up for half a mile along the service road. Somewhere nearby, no doubt obscured under more thick netting, crouched the SA-8 currently tracking him.

McQuade's eyes dropped to the distance countdown on his HUD. In unison, the two Vipers banked into a hard right turn, racing towards the forest and flying so low that the tall tips of the treetops seemed to scrape their underbellies.

Hernandez maneuvered into a ten-degree low angle, low-drag attack. McQuade pulled the nose of his Viper up to a simultaneous thirty-degree climb angle, the two Vipers diverging as the fuel depot grew in size and detail. As soon as McQuade began his climb, he thumped the aircraft's chaff dispenser, filling the air behind him with thousands of shredded aluminum pieces to divert the enemy SAM's guidance systems.

"Spartacus One is in!" Hernandez thumbed his mike button and rolled his Viper in on the target. The fuel dump was at their right nine o'clock. The Viper swooped down like a silver bird of prey and at the precise moment released the MK-84 attached to the pylon beneath his left wing.

The huge bomb landed squarely in the middle of the vast forest clearing and exploded, causing cataclysmic damage. Orange columns of flame spewed into the air from ruptured underground storage tanks, gushing like fountains and spraying fuel for hundreds of yards in every direction. The small control building that regulated the pumping burst into flames, and a dozen fuel trucks closest to the initial explosion were engulfed in fireballs. Hundreds of Russian soldiers were killed or injured in the chain of secondary explosions that shook the earth and filled the sky with a huge thunder cloud of black smoke. Within seconds, the flames had spread to the nearby forest as escaping diesel and gasoline ran like blazing rivers through the tinder-dry undergrowth.

McQuade did not see the massive explosion caused by Hernandez's bomb, but he heard and sensed the vast detonation shudder the air. Instead, his eyes were locked onto his HUD as his Viper continued to climb. Smoke boiled black and billowing beneath his fighter as he rocketed through four thousand feet. He counted down the seconds, feeling vulnerable and exposed, acutely aware that the enemy SAM site was hunting him. He fired off a second cloud of chaff as the Viper reached five thousand feet. Instantly McQuade made a sharp turn towards the target, pulling five Gs as he lined his fighter up for the attack.

"Spartacus Two is in!"

He pulled wings level with his nose in a twenty-degree dive and cast his eyes ahead to visually acquire the target. It was impossible to miss. The entire fuel depot seemed engulfed in flames. Even during the scant few seconds he had to register the devastation he saw two more explosions, both on the fringes of the woods. He hoped they were enemy SAM sites blowing up. He pushed the missile step button on the fighter's control stick to call up the CCIP (continuously computed impact point) pipper and the bomb steering line that guided the pilot accurately to target. Still descending, he jinked the Viper left, then back to the right until the pipper on the display was directly over the center of the blazing fuel depot. McQuade thumbed the pickle button. He heard a loud *'thump!'* and the Viper's wings rocked as the MK-84 attached to the underside of his left wing suddenly fell away.

The Viper seemed instantly lighter and more agile to his touch. He put the fighter into a brutal five-G climb until the nose of the aircraft drew level with the horizon and was turned towards his egress heading. Hernandez's Viper was nowhere to be seen.

McQuade descended back down to five hundred feet and peered hard ahead. He was flying almost due north, skimming the canopy of the forest. Hernandez's Viper appeared as a silver speck at his left two o'clock. McQuade accelerated until the two fighters had rejoined, flying abeam of each other, five thousand yards apart.

The two Vipers searched the surrounding sky for enemy fighters. By now the Russians would be alerted to their presence. McQuade's eyes kept darting to his radar scope which remained ominously silent. He was breathing hard. The cramped confines of the cockpit smelled of sweat.

Beneath the two fighters the terrain changed quickly; forest canopy gave way to open fields and a sudden criss-crossing network of roads. Houses and then small settlements flashed beneath their wings. On the horizon the skyline grew dark and grey with the clutter of a city skyline crouched beneath an oppressive blanket of drifting black smoke. The big engine of the Viper vibrated through the floor of the cockpit and throbbed against McQuade's heels as the American fighters dashed towards the eastern outskirts of Kiev and their second mission target.

*

As the two Vipers raced on towards the outskirts of Kiev, flying level at a thousand feet, the cloud and smoke around them began to thicken. Hernandez peered through the scrims of haze, looking for the north-south highway that would guide them to their target. McQuade tilted his head back and checked the sky above, but the air was clotted with black smears of smoke. It was like flying through soup. McQuade's Viper began to buck and shudder, then pitched violently sideways in turbulent air. The pilot swore and wrenched the fighter back on course. His face was damp with sweat, his heart thumping against the cage of his chest.

Hernandez began a gradual descent and McQuade shadowed him. They dropped down to seven hundred feet and suddenly the ragged cloud layer lifted. They were skimming along at five hundred and fifty knots.

McQuade could see nothing above him other than the impenetrable layer of dark smoky haze. His entire world telescoped down to the ground, racing in a blur beneath the nose of his jet.

Ahead, the city of Kiev emerged like a solid wall of tall smoking buildings, grey and bleak in the filtered light. Then the highway appeared about a mile off the nose of Hernandez's fighter; a dark grey slash against the brown and green patch-worked landscape. Hernandez made a gentle course correction and McQuade followed, still wrestling with the controls of his aircraft and kicking hard at the rudder to fight the sideways skid of the wind.

Houses flashed past, most of them bombed smoldering ruins. The ground by the side of the highway turned blackened and charred. They flew over a column of destroyed trucks, scattered haphazardly across the highway. The blacktop was littered with debris, the vehicles blown to fragments and burned. McQuade saw a clump of dark crumpled shapes on the fringes of the chaos and knew they were dead bodies.

Suddenly the sky around the two Vipers changed color. The light flashed red and orange as tracer fire blew past their cockpits. The air around the fighters seemed to quiver with the *'crump!'* of multiple explosions. McQuade jinked his fighter instinctively, pulling G-forces as he tossed his Viper from side to side. His radar warning receiver filled with a hash of figure '8' icons, telling him that somewhere nearby multiple Gecko missile systems had locked on to his approach. The warning warble in his headset became a constant rising clamor. Both pilots pumped out a veil of chaff and flares. McQuade gritted his teeth and fought the instinctive urge to flee: to hit his afterburner and climb for the illusory safety of altitude. The sound inside his head was a silent scream of alarm.

An explosion beyond his left wing flashed bright red, flecked with orange tongues of flame. The force of the blast rocked the fighter violently sideways and his head cracked against the canopy. A mushroom of smoke bloomed overhead and was lost in the blanket of clouds, then another searing white flash of light lit the cockpit up.

The sound of the threat warning receiver became strident. McQuade flicked his eyes sideways and caught another glimpse of the small scope. It was a jumble of flashing green numbers – too many warnings to discern them all individually.

McQuade's gaze flicked over to the distance measuring display on his HUD. The two Vipers banked into a hard left turn, veering away from the ribbon of highway and skimming over a precinct of low-rise drab apartments. The buildings looked like prison blocks, arranged in squares around a tiny patch of green grass. Most of the buildings had been hit by artillery fire and were still smoldering. Two destroyed tanks stood amongst the rubble.

The two fighters swung onto their target approach path. Beneath them the ground seemed to light up with twinkling white and orange lights of gunfire. Tracer reached out for them from every direction.

The fighters were still six miles from target. Hernandez pushed the nose of his Viper down and rammed the throttle forward, firing out more bundles of chaff. McQuade followed his flight leader. He had the strange sensation that he was not moving, that he was marking time in the grey void. The cacophony of noise outside the canopy seemed suddenly muted. Even the warble of the radar warning alarm and the howl of the fighter's engine seemed subdued. But his heart pounded like a thumping drum.

The two fighters sank down to three hundred feet and into a patch of suddenly still air. It lasted for just three seconds. Then the landscape beneath them became filled with parked Russian vehicles; BMP-3s and tanks and trucks. They were arranged in neat rows across a wide mud-churned field, all painted in camouflage colors.

A white trail of smoke lifted off from the ground.

"Shoulder launched SAM!" Hernandez saw a corkscrewing trail of smoke as it dashed towards them at blinding speed. Both pilots stabbed their thumbs at the countermeasure-dispense switch on their sticks as fast as they could to flood the air with a sequence of chaff and flares designed to disorientate infrared and radar-guided missiles. Two more white trails of smoke rose from the ground. McQuade brought his fighter wings level and pumped more chaff into the air.

In a pounding heartbeat the target was upon them – a nondescript building he recognized from the photos at the intelligence briefing. The structure was a single-story brick sprawl. It looked like it might once have been a community meeting hall or perhaps a police station. McQuade swallowed hard and flexed his fingers. Inside his gloves his hands were a cold clammy sweat. When he spoke across the radio, his voice sounded oddly high-pitched and hoarse.

"Spartacus Two is in!"

The two pilots had reversed order and mode of attack for the second target. McQuade tilted the nose of his Viper forward until he was into a ten-degree low angle, low-drag attack and flew straight at the target.

He saw Hernandez's Viper off his wing suddenly peel off and climb upwards out of the corner of his eye and then he focused all his attention on lining up the target. He squeezed the missile step button on the control stick to activate the CCIP pipper and the bomb steering line on his HUD, then twitched the stick until the pipper was over the center of the building's peaked roof. When he thumbed the pickle button the MK-84 beneath his right wing suddenly fell away. Free of its two thousand pound burden, the Viper became light and agile as a swallow. McQuade pulled hard back on the stick and sheered away as he climbed, tilting the fighter onto its side as he looked for his egress point and tried to peer back over his shoulder to watch the fall of the bomb.

The MK-84 struck the headquarters building flush, obliterating the target in a *'whoosh!'* of fire and billowing smoke. The thunder of the explosion blotted out every other sound for an instant, shaking the air. Exhilaration, terror and relief all fused together into a choke of emotion. McQuade leaned his head back against the ejection seat and let the cocktail of sensations wash over him, then lit the Viper's afterburner, clawing at the smoke-filled sky for altitude and speed.

"Spartacus One is in!"

Hernandez came out of his climb and swooped, releasing his bomb slightly left of target to complete the simultaneous attack. The MK-84 contained almost a thousand pounds of Tritanol explosive filler and a thousand pounds of steel. An instant before the bomb exploded the steel casing was designed to expand to twice its normal size, creating a crater up to fifty-feet wide. Everything and everyone within half a mile of ground zero was killed instantly.

The egress point for the mission was to the north east. The two Vipers rejoined at five thousand feet, several miles beyond the outskirts of the city. Hernandez led the fighters into a gentle climb. McQuade took a deep breath and pulled the oxygen mask from his face. His jaw ached and his body twitched with the after-effects of adrenalin. Inside his flight gloves his fingers trembled uncontrollably. He wondered if he would ever stop shaking.

Chapter 2:

The two Vipers flew on, gradually turning towards the west and climbing to thirty thousand feet, their flight path a long lazy hook in the sky that would carry them clear of enemy forces and bring them back onto a heading for Lutsk Air Base.

McQuade wriggled in his seat and tried to remain focused on flying in formation. After the fear-induced adrenalin-surge of combat, cruising in calm air seemed an anti-climax. Visually he scanned his radar scope for enemy fighters, but behind the visor of his helmet, his mind frantically replayed every second of the attack on the Russian Army headquarters. He saw it all again, slowed down, as though only through recall could he process the moment. He remembered the wicked sound of gunfire flying past his canopy and the brilliant burning flashes of light. He remembered the way the Viper bucked violently as explosions shook the air around him. He had been scared in the air before – but he had never come this close to white-hot terror.

Outside the cockpit the cloud cover across northern Ukraine had scattered, revealing battle scarred fields far below lit by pinpricks of fire. McQuade reached for the air-to-ground button on his up-front control, activating the Viper's ground-map radar. Two bright lights appear directly ahead. The aircraft's system was unable to identify the threat. McQuade frowned. He guessed it was most likely an SA-8 'Gecko'; a mobile, low-altitude, short-range SAM system in service with the Russian military. The SA-8 had a ceiling of about nineteen thousand feet.

"Spartacus One, two bright lights at twelve o'clock," he radioed.

"One is no joy," Hernandez replied. "Identified?"

"Negative. Best guess is SA-8s."

There was a long pause. McQuade imagined Hernandez scanning his own fighter's ground-map radar. He re-checked his readout and realized with a small start that both bright lights had disappeared.

"Spartacus Two has lost contact."

"Roger that," Hernandez grunted and the two Vipers flew on, cruising towards their next steerpoint.

Suddenly a new, unfamiliar voice broke across the radio in both Vipers cockpits, the tone urgent, struggling to remain professional and restrained.

"All players! All players! This is Desert Fox on Guard, calling for Emergency Close Air Support. All CAS-capable flights report. Emergency CAS situation in progress. Report your availability on Yankee two-two."

Ron Hernandez frowned and stared down at the stack of mission materials he wore strapped to his thigh. The folder was filled with a list of call signs, maps and a comms card detailing every Allied frequency. Hernandez had never heard of Yankee two-two.

Hernandez checked his fuel status readout in the HUD and frowned again. The green symbology in the center of his display was flashing. The F-16 wasn't well-suited to close air support, but the unwritten rule of air combat was whenever troops on the ground needed help, every available fighter was obliged to fly to the rescue.

Still Hernandez hesitated. He felt certain a Ukraine fighter would be operating somewhere in the sky nearby. The Ukrainian Air Force had taken a severe beating from the Russians in the opening phases of the conflict and been forced to withdraw to air bases in the south of the country. But their handful of operational MiG-29s were still flying missions. Surely one of the Ukraine jets was aloft and would respond…

Surely…

The two Vipers closed to within five hundred feet of each other and Hernandez initiated a visual fuel check by making a fist with his thumb extended and pantomimed a drinking motion, lifting his hand towards his mouth. McQuade responded with his own hand signals to reflect his fuel status. He was a few hundred pounds lower than Hernandez; typical because the wingman needed to use extra energy to maintain his position.

Hernandez counted to ten.

Desert Fox came on the air again, this time the caller's tone was near frantic. Hernandez couldn't identify the accent; it wasn't an American voice. "All players! All CAS-capable flights report on Yankee two-two. Emergency Close Air Support required. Repeat. All players! All players…!"

Hernandez felt a shameful stab of guilt for his delayed response and keyed his radio.

"Desert Fox this is Spartacus One. We are two by Fox One Six each with a thousand rounds of 20mm and eleven minutes of playtime before bingo fuel. Over."

A Ukraine company of infantry reserves fighting in the ruins of northern Kiev's outskirts were on the brink of being overwhelmed by a battalion of Russian troops, supported by BMP-2s. Desert Fox put Hernandez in direct comms with the captain of the Ukraine soldiers, call sign Wolverine.

Hernandez keyed McQuade on the radio while the call to the beleaguered troops on the ground was being patched through. The two Vipers pulled into a steep right-hand turn towards the capital, sinking down to twenty thousand feet and increasing speed.

*

"Wolverine! Wolverine! Spartacus flight of two Vipers checking in."

The initial communication between a CAS fighter and a JTAC typically started with the fighter pilot giving a 'fighter-to-FAC' briefing. Pilots referred to the mnemonic MNPOPA which stood for mission number, number of aircraft, playtime, ordnance, particulars and abort code. Hernandez shared the details over the radio.

For a moment there was just a long fraught static silence.

"Wolverine! This is Spartacus flight… report your type and position."

"Roger, Spartacus," the voice was thickly accented and sounded harried. "Thank God you responded. We are a Company of Ukrainian reserve infantry under direct and deadly assault from Russian infantry and PCs. We occupy a row of buildings near Park Kyn'-Grust on the outskirts of Kiev. We are on the *south* side of Kobzarska Street." Wolverine rattled off the unit's MGRS (Military Grid Reference System). The MGRS was a two-dimensional grid that accurately identified the unit's location to a ten-meter square. There was an abrupt pause for several seconds, filled with a staccato of automatic weapons firing followed by the rattle of an explosion. When Wolverine spoke again, the voice on the radio was rattled and sharp with rising panic. "The Russians are in the park to the north of our position. We are in houses south east of Vynohradar Reservoir, in Vynohradar District. Give me everything you've got on the woods immediately to our north. I am setting off red smoke now. You are cleared hot!"

Hernandez felt a fist of apprehension punch him hard in the guts. It was standard procedure during a CAS operation for the ground force seeking assistance to issue a 9-line sitrep of their position which was typically followed by confirmation from JTAC (Joint Terminal Air Controller) before ordnance could be dropped. The procedure was a critical step to ensure the pilots knew exactly where the friendly forces were located and where the enemy were concentrated. By abandoning procedural steps, Hernandez got a sense of the urgent life-or-death threat facing the Ukraine infantry. The fact that Wolverine was not concerned with adhering to procedure emphasized the sheer desperation of their circumstances.

Hernandez put the nose of his Viper down and dropped through ten thousand feet. He ordered McQuade to orbit the area and maintain his altitude then got back on his radio to the Captain of the Ukrainian infantry.

"Wolverine! Spartacus One is attacking from the northeast in ninety seconds."

"Hurry, Spartacus One! Firing off more smoke now."

The Viper dropped through seven thousand feet and emerged through a thin band of wispy cloud. The scene below Hernandez's fighter was one of utter devastation. The entire northern district of Kiev had been flattened to grey rubble by Russian artillery and bombing raids. The only buildings that remained were deserted shell-shattered skeletons. Apartment buildings stood as empty fire-blackened carcasses, their windows blown out, surrounded by high mounds of rubble. Most of the buildings Hernandez flew over had lost their roofs; many were still burning or smoldering black smoke into the sky. Walls had collapsed and beneath the debris were parked cars. Some buildings had been completely obliterated; others had been struck glancing blows so the wreckage stood as a crumbling ruin. The few trees he could see were blackened stumps. Vast overlapping craters of muddy stagnant water showed where artillery rounds had fallen and blinked reflected light up at him as he flashed overhead.

Hernandez felt his cheeks begin to burn and his empty guts became gripped by spasms. In his head the battle clock began to count down so that the passage of time seemed to slow. Minute details came into sharp focus. He saw a church in the distance, its green copper-clad spire still standing, but leaning drunkenly at an angle. The rest of the grand old building had been shot-holed by artillery shells, the southwest wall collapsed and trailing grey smoke. Just beyond the church was a small community park. The grass was scorched, the playground equipment melted into obscene twisted wreckage. Two shell craters pock-marked the edge of the clearing, leaving ugly brown scars of thrown dirt across a nearby footpath.

Suddenly a mist of red smoke trailed into the sky, far off in the distance, rising above the buildings to stand against the bleak grey backdrop of clouds. Hernandez made a minor adjustment, twitching the Viper a little to the right. He could see a mottled expanse of brown trees, denuded of their leaves. There was movement in the woods; dark ugly steel shapes surrounded by black specks that were running men.

"Spartacus One, hurry!" Wolverine's voice broke across the radio again, thick with panic and desperation.

Hernandez fought the overwhelming urge to recklessly dive into the fight. He keyed the mike and kept his voice dispassionate and clinical.

"Wolverine I am three-zero seconds from attack run. Confirm your position."

The reply from the Ukrainian Captain on the other end of the radio was instantaneous. He barked the MGRS co-ordinates again and repeated the list of physical markers. "Give me everything you've got on the woods immediately to our north. You are cleared hot! Repeat. You are cleared hot!"

"Confirm there are no friendly troops on the road north of your location. Confirm your men are all in the buildings on the south side of the road."

"Affirmative!"

Hernandez switched his Master Arm switch to 'on' and activated the fighter's HUD film.

On the right-side MFD display inside the cockpit, Hernandez set the controls for 'gun strafe' preparing the M61A1 20mm Vulcan cannon for action. The weapon fired up to six thousand rounds per minute. He diverted his attention to the air speed indicator and saw the fighter was traveling at four hundred and fifty knots. He set the Viper into a twenty-degree dive and felt himself begin to tense. He leveled the fighter out at a thousand feet and closed the Viper's speed brakes. The aircraft's momentum slowly bled away until it was traveling at four hundred knots.

The scene around the woods came sharply into focus as he dashed towards the target. He could identify at least a dozen Russian BMPs and over a hundred enemy troops. They were moving forward in loose formation, under the cover of the PCs machine guns. Across the crater-damaged ribbon of road stood a line of bomb-shattered houses and a couple of small apartment blocks. Beyond them the Vynohradar Reservoir glinted sunlight.

The F-16 dropped to five hundred feet, and Hernandez shoved the throttle and the fighter's nose forward.

"Spartacus One, hurry!" Wolverine cried. The radio message cut in and out with static. "The Russians have reached the far side of the road. We are seconds from being overrun."

Hernandez's heart thumped wildly. The cockpit seemed a chaos of noise and rattles and blinking lights. He glanced sideways at his Radar Warning Receiver and saw the screen was mercifully blank of immediate dangers. He lined up the green reticle and watched the path marker in the center of his HUD. At the top of the marker was the bore-sight gun cross, locked onto the distant woods. The reticle slid up the HUD display and then suddenly overlapped the target point. Hernandez thumbed the trigger and felt the Viper's airframe shudder and rock sideways.

A line of flashing bullets reached out from the F-16 and streaked towards the edge of the woods. Hernandez saw the brutal punch of his rounds fly home, striking Russian BMP-2s and scattering the infantry. He was over the target for just four seconds. In the background, the cockpit's automated 'Bitchin' Betty' began to chant in a synthetic warning voice, *"Altitude! Altitude!"*

Hernandez pulled the Viper out of its dive and flashed past the woods. He threw the fighter into a sharp right-hand turn, tilting the agile aircraft onto its wingtip. His radio exploded to life.

"Delta Hotel! Delta Hotel!" The Ukrainian Captain's voice was pathetic with gratitude. "Direct hits!"

Hernandez completed his turn and keyed his mike. "Wolverine, Spartacus One is off to the west. Coming back for one last attack before bingo and RTB. Over."

"Roger, Spartacus One. Target position is unchanged."

Hernandez brought his fighter around in a tight G-turn, just two hundred feet above the ground. He leveled the wings and leaned left until he could see the narrow suburban street past the HUD display. He jiggled the stick a couple of times until he was lined up. The ground flashed beneath the nose of the Viper in a brown and grey blur. His speed was nearing five hundred knots; it was too fast to maneuver, and it was too late to make corrections.

To add to his stress, Wolverine's voice came back on the radio, loud in his helmet's earpiece.

"Spartacus One... out the infantry... BMPs... woods!" the message broke into fragments, fractured by static and obliterated by the percussive sound of multiple explosions. Hernandez shut the distraction from his mind and concentrated all his attention on the thin ribbon of road racing towards him. He could see four Russian BMPs on the fringe of the woods; their turret-mounted machine guns providing overwatch for a platoon of advancing infantry. Some of the troops were running across the road, others had reached the far side of the street and were in amongst the buildings.

The distance closed rapidly. Hernandez bunted the fighter's nose over and coaxed the aiming circle pipper on his HUD until it wobbled up the screen of his display towards the target.

Come on! He twitched the stick and the Viper's wings rocked. The aircraft was skittishly agile, responding instantly to his slightest touch. The pipper began to rise up the HUD, but off to the left. *Come on!*

He could see Russian infantry stop suddenly and turn their heads towards him. He swooped down like a bird of prey. Some of the soldiers threw up their automatic weapons and sprayed fire at the approaching Viper. One of the BMPs turrets turned and a stream of flashing green tracer rounds arced up from the ground to intercept him. The fire flew wide to the left, but began to correct as the gunner adjusted his aim. Out of the corner of his eye he saw a Russian soldier drop to his knee. The soldier had something mounted on his shoulder...

Come on!

The pipper wiggled towards the path marker line and then finally the target and the pipper converged and overlapped. Hernandez felt a sudden savage elation.

He squeezed the trigger with his curled forefinger.

The M61 Vulcan Gatling-style rotary cannon roared.

The cannon fired one hundred rounds every second. Hernandez held the trigger down for a short lethal burst.

Dark figures scattered back into the illusory cover of the woods. Some men threw themselves behind the steel shelter of the BMPs and tried to bury their bodies under dirt. Some were cruelly cut down where they stood, shredded by the heavy impact of machine gun fire. One Russian officer was struck by a hail of spitting bullets and disintegrated in a pink mist of blood, his body dismembered by the monstrous impact of multiple hits. Chunks of blacktop were gouged out of the road as the air above the woods filled with the screaming thunder of the fighter's swooping passage. Two of the BMPs took hits, but Hernandez had no idea how badly they had been damaged. Both vehicles disappeared behind a haze of churned up dirt and flashing sparks.

As soon as he was past the target, he pulled the Viper up into a steep climb, pulling six Gs and accelerating as he fired off clouds of chaff and flares to mask his escape. His eyes flicked to the Viper's 'rounds remaining' counter and then to the radar altimeter. He had a couple of hundred rounds left – not enough to justify another attack. He kicked the rudder hard to throw off the enemy's aim.

"Wolverine, Spartacus One is off to the west. I am bingo and Winchester. RTB. Good luck!"

He turned his attention to the Viper's air-to-air radar and detected Spartacus Two. McQuade was flying a racetrack pattern at ten thousand feet, holding station over the battleground and scanning the hostile skies for enemy fighters. The two Vipers made contact, and as McQuade pulled out of his pattern and began to steer towards the west, Hernandez continued his climb and altered his course to rejoin. He felt physically exhausted. His butt was numb; his flight suit soaked with sweat. He felt fatigued, like he was coming down from a drug-induced high, or waking up with a hang-over the morning after a wild night.

The two F-16s rendezvoused over the western outskirts of Kiev. The pilots eyeballed each other across the void, flying parallel to each other. On the far horizon a scar of dark clouds was building. The impending storm lay low against the ground, a thin black smudge – but even as they watched, it seemed to grow – spreading across the blue skyline, darkening and building upon itself as it rose.

Suddenly an SA-8 symbol appeared in the upper left quadrant of Hernandez's RWR scope and a warning buzz filled his headset.

Hernandez keyed his mike.

"Spartacus Two, Mud eight, one-five-zero, medium."

"No joy, One," McQuade's tone was frustrated. Hernandez looked across and saw his wingman leaning forward against his cockpit harness, fiddling with his Viper's controls. Then the buzz turned into a sharp series of warning beeps.

The SA-8 had launched! Missiles were in the air.

The hunters had just become the hunted.

*

"Spartacus One, launch right five o'clock!" Hernandez radioed frantically. He sat, twisted awkwardly against his harness, peering over his shoulder and down through wisping scrims of white cloud, looking for the tell-tale grey streak of smoke that would identify the inbound missile.

McQuade took a death-grip on his stick and began toggling off bundles of glittering chaff as he put his F-16 into a series of jinking weaves. A few seconds later a second SA-8 appeared on his scope, followed by another launch indicator.

"Spartacus Two, second launch, five o'clock right!"

Against all reason McQuade put his fighter's nose down and went into a dive, plunging a thousand feet in a few seconds and then climbing again sharply into a vertical 'S'. But the aircraft had lost energy due to the steepness of the climb. Its speed slowed to three hundred knots. Through the top of his bubble canopy, McQuade could see Hernandez's Viper jinking across the sky.

Hernandez was looking down on McQuade, frowning heavily into his face mask, sweeping the ground far below for the first hint of an approaching missile.

At last he saw the first vapor trail, rising on a serpentine track of grey smoke, coming up from the earth's mottled surface fast, almost directly behind him.

"Spartacus One, tally! Con my six!"

A few moments later he detected the second launch. A programmed voice built in to the plane's computer system sounded loud in Hernandez's headset. *"Counter. Counter."*

Both aircraft banked right to put the approaching missiles on their starboard side, still separated by almost a thousand feet of sky. McQuade peered over the sill of his canopy; the missile was dashing towards him at twice the speed of sound. A liquid, icy terror washed through his veins.

The first SA-8 missile detonated between the two aircraft in a brilliant flash of white-yellow light and a mushroom cloud of smoke. The second missile locked on to McQuade's Viper and closed on the aircraft quickly.

Communications protocol between the two F-16 pilots was replaced with urgent barked instructions.

"Spartacus Two, Break right! SAM your six o'clock low!" Hernandez yelled into his oxygen mask, his throat hoarse with horror. "Break! Break! Break!" and he saw the younger pilot react with cat-like reflexes, his response on the stick and rudder almost instant. The Viper flipped onto its wingtip and rolled to the right like a boxer swaying out of reach of a well-swung punch.

McQuade put the Viper into a near-vertical climb and felt himself pushed deep into the ejector seat by the sudden crush of G-forces. Slowly his speed began to bleed away. He twisted round and craned his neck over his shoulder. The missile wavered in and out of sight behind the fighter's great fiery engine, closing fast.

"Dive! Dive! Dive!"

McQuade flipped out of his steep climb. The Viper hung in the air for a moment at the zenith of its ascent, and then put its nose down and plunged like a stone. The missile swerved in the sky and flashed past the Viper's left side. McQuade saw the missile at the last instant and was consumed by a sudden sense of fatalistic dismay. Inside the Russian missile the proximity fuse detonated automatically in a brusque burst of orange flame, tearing chunks out of the cropped-delta wing of the Viper.

*

The impact inside the Viper's cockpit was like being hit by a runaway train. In the blink of an eye the Viper was transformed from a sleek agile bird of prey into a steel coffin plummeting towards earth. The aircraft seemed to slew in the air for a fraction of a second; the stick in McQuade's white-knuckled fist jerking.

McQuade's first reaction was paralyzing fear. He sat stunned, thrown so violently forward against his safety harness that the straps sawed painfully against his body and scraped skin from his shoulders. A tiny fragment of debris had penetrated the bubble canopy. Howling icy wind came blasting through the hole, filling the interior with dust.

His vision cleared and his mind became sharp. The Viper began tumbling down the sky like a leaf, turning end over end. He wrenched his head sideways and saw the damaged wing disintegrating under the tremendous pressure of its slewing free-fall. He fought against the stick and kicked at the rudder pedal, trying to bring the fighter under control. The altimeter in his HUD began winding down like a doomsday clock.

In his ear he could hear 'Bitchin' Betty', the Viper's automated warning voice, over the sounds of a dozen alarms and buzzers. The fighter's airframe began to shudder violently around him as though the aircraft was being shaken like a petulant giant's toy. His head cracked hard against the side of the canopy and a coppery taste of blood filled his mouth. The fighter began to pitch and roll violently.

Then the Viper seemed to lose all momentum and die in the sky.

"Engine fire! Engine fire!" 'Bitchin' Betty's' voice seemed to rise in urgent volume, slashing through the fraught chaos.

"Christ!" McQuade felt a knot of cold, clammy fear slide in his guts. "Dear God! Please don't let me die – please don't let me die!"

He glanced at the altimeter and saw he was at four thousand feet. He had fallen almost six thousand feet in a matter of seconds. He wrestled with the stick, trying to flatten and counter the aircraft's wild unbalanced spins. Another shattered chunk of wing tore from the mangled airframe and blew past the canopy. The Viper seemed to groan like a mortally wounded beast in its death throes.

"The engine is FOD'd," he reported on Comm 2, his voice rising in hysteria and panic. "Left wing severely damaged and breaking up!"

Ron Hernandez watched the Viper die from the cockpit of his fighter, overcome with gut-wrenching grief. He followed the stricken aircraft down as it fell from the sky, appalled. He saw small fragments breaking away from the aircraft's wing and then a larger twisted chunk tore off the plane, cartwheeling through the air. He stabbed at his mike switch and his voice in his own ears sounded tense with alarm.

"Eject Two! Eject! Eject!"

*

McQuade choked down a surge of paralyzing fear as the Viper began to disintegrate around him, shaking his body ruthlessly about the cockpit. Through a blur of dust and confusion he groped for the yellow and black striped handle attached to his seat, stamped with the words 'pull to eject'. It was harder than he had ever imagined; a fight against positive and negative G's as the F-16 plummeted down the sky.

Time seemed to slow. McQuade had an instant to fret that his canopy would not open, or that the seat would not eject him clear of the debris. He saw the ground coming up to meet him, turning over and over through a continuous spin.

The fingers of his left hand wrapped around the thick yellow handle and he heaved with all his might.

Ejecting from a fighter at over four hundred knots comes with its own gruesome risks. McQuade had heard the macabre mess room stories; tales of pilots suffering crippling vertebral fractures, neck injuries, spinal damage, and hideously fractured legs. The odds were good that if he survived the trauma of being rocketed out of the aircraft, he wouldn't survive uninjured.

The F-16's canopy exploded off the cockpit and went cartwheeling across the sky. The rocket under the pilot's seat fired automatically, hurtling McQuade into the cold howling air.

The shrieking wind tore mercilessly at him. The force of its velocity ripped his flight helmet clean off his head and crushed the blood vessels in his face. He screamed in pain. The ferocious wind seared his lungs. He felt like he was dying and in his mind he began to chant desperate prayers to a God he didn't believe in.

A small drogue chute activated, designed to stabilize the pilot as he began to fall through the sky. Two seconds later the main chute deployed and the heavy pilot seat fell away.

McQuade had ejected at just over three thousand feet. He knew he had only a few seconds before he would hit the ground. He moved his arms and legs, checking for injuries, then stared down between his boots at the earth rising up to meet him. A gust of wind caught the chute, dragging him further east.

He began drifting back over the western outskirts of Kiev. The terrain below seemed a scatter of bomb-ruined buildings, boiling smoke and twisted debris. Avalanches of rubble lay across the roads and at the corners of collapsed buildings. In the distance he could hear the far-away rumble of artillery shells exploding and the higher-pitched chatter of automatic gunfire. The entire devastated skyline was smudged with columns of black smoke.

As he descended, the surrounds grew stark in detail. He was drifting towards a suburban intersection. At one corner he saw the remains of an apartment block, the windows blackened by fire and much of the interior gutted. The roof had collapsed, crumbling the south-side wall. On the opposite side of the road lay a small clearing of grass with a park bench and the blackened stump of a tree.

The north side of the intersection was dominated by what he suspected was a church. He peered down between his dangling legs as the ground rushed up to meet him. Instead of a steeple, the building had several curious domes, topped with small crosses. The entire elaborate structure was set on a clearing of ground, surrounded by a high stone wall. In the far corner, close to what appeared to be a service gate joined to a narrow side alley, he saw several grey slabbed cemetery plots.

About a mile to the west lay the tangled wreckage of his Viper, engulfed in fire and a pyre of black smoke, burning like a beacon. It had crashed into the side of a bomb-ruined building, reigniting smoldering fires in the charred and blackened debris. McQuade knew that if he was to survive, he would have to clear the area and find shelter – quickly. Within minutes the Russian Army would be swarming around the site, trying to capture him. An image, unbidden, flashed across his imagination. He saw himself in a dark cold prison cell, bruised and beaten, his hands cuffed behind his back. The thought gave him renewed determination.

His mind flashed back over his training as the ground rushed up to meet him. *Legs together, ankles, knees, hips side roll…*

He hit the ground hard, landing within the perimeter of the church. His knees buckled and his whole body seemed to collapse. He rolled across the grass. The parachute enveloped him like a soft silken blanket. His head felt brutally bruised and swollen as though he had been beaten with a club. His mouth was filled with blood; his lips thick and rubbery. He scrambled to his feet, released his parachute, and stuffed the bundle of nylon beneath rubble from the bomb-damaged perimeter wall. He staggered unsteadily to the service gate. Through the grille of steel bars he had a view across a bleak war-devastated wasteland.

To the south, maybe five hundred yards away through a cratered stretch of road and a litter of burned-out cars, he saw a cluster of ruined apartment blocks. He pushed open the gate and began to run, limping a little against the pain of a sprained ankle. His teeth felt loose, and his breath sawed painfully across his throat. The facial swelling made his head pound and flop heavily on his neck. His vision began to blur and he had to stop, exposed and in the open for long seconds, to catch his breath and steady his trembling legs.

He remembered his survival training in the mountains of Spokane, Washington, and realized he had to shift into escape and evade mode. He made a quick inventory; he had his 9mm M9 Beretta and his survival vest that contained a small radio, a flare, camouflage paint, a GPS, waterproof matches, a tourniquet, military compass, a magnesium fire starter and infrared tape. It wasn't a lot. He needed maps and water and food and a place to hide before the Russians began hunting him.

Low overhead, Hernandez's Viper came darting in from the west. McQuade paused long enough to wave his arms above his head. The fighter jet hurtled by, the air seeming to quiver violently in its wake. Hernandez waggled his wings and then pulled up into a steep vertical climb, gaining altitude before turning tightly and flashing away to the west, heading back towards Lutsk Air Base.

Once within the shadows of the bombed apartments, McQuade fumbled for the handheld radio in a pocket of his survival vest. He tore the radio free from its plastic wrapping and broadcast.

"Anyone. Spartacus Two," the words through his swollen lips sounded thick and slurred.

Static.

Chapter 3:

McQuade crouched low and tried to orientate himself. A bomb-ruined apartment complex stood to his left, the roof disintegrated, all the windows shattered, the outer walls blackened with soot and fire damage. A section of a brick wall that led to an enclosed courtyard had collapsed across the narrow road, littering the street with debris and dust. Hidden beneath the rubble lay the crushed remains of a small car that had been gutted by fire.

Amidst the ruins McQuade saw broken furniture, children's toys and items of clothing; everything destroyed or left blackened and melted by flames. The street looked like a demolition site after the work of a wrecking ball. Broken timber beams and slabs of concrete lay in high piles around mounds of shattered roof tiles and sheets of rusted corrugated iron.

He drew the M9 Beretta from the shoulder holster inside his flight suit and rose cautiously to his feet. He turned his head in a slow circle. A little to his right, at the end of a rubble-strewn laneway, he saw a brick wall that had been built between two houses. Both the houses had been destroyed by Russian artillery, but the wall joining them remained. There was only a narrow gap in the bricks, but McQuade could make out the shape of a second wall beyond the first.

He approached the wall carefully. The laneway on either side was lined with sheets of graffiti-covered corrugated iron fencing that rose above his head, so he felt cornered and vulnerable. He imagined a Russian sniper watching him through his telescopic sight from the window of a ruined building. The thought made him cringe, and he tried to shrink himself into a smaller target. His leaden feet stumbled over a handful of broken bricks and the noise of the scuffle sounded as loud as an alarm in his ears.

Halfway along the alley McQuade stopped and strained to listen. He could hear small sounds of movement further away to his right, and in the background came the constant muted *'crump!'* of faraway artillery fire. Somewhere behind him a shot rang out and he turned his head in alarm, but saw no sign of pursuit, though he knew the Russians must be closing on him. The realization filled him with a fresh prickle of fear.

He reached the brick wall and peered through the narrow opening. Beyond was a second, lower wall, that ended at a spill of fallen rubble about twenty yards to his left. McQuade dropped down to a crouch and crawled forward until he reached the mound of rubble, then lifted his head slowly.

The view beyond his hiding place was a landscape of desolation. Across an open space that had perhaps once been a children's playground, he saw more demolished buildings, many of them still billowing black smoke into the grey hazed sky. The sidewalks were cluttered with mounds of rubble and the road was scattered with parked cars, each of them crushed and burned out by the relentless bombing. The scene looked utterly holocaustic, made worse by the pungent smells of smoke, rotting food and the sickly-sweet stench of corruption that wafted on the breeze.

McQuade's heart thumped in his chest so hard that the sound seemed to echo in his ears as he studied the scene of devastation. He shifted his weight, coming up onto his haunches and estimated the distance to the nearest ruined building. He guessed it was fifty yards, across open, rubble-strewn ground.

"It's now or never." He had not meant to speak aloud, and the sound of his own voice made him flinch. He tensed himself like an athlete on the blocks and cast a last wary glance across the open ground. Russian troops could be in any of the buildings, or lying in wait in one of the bomb craters that pock-marked the field. He licked his lips and stared out across the wasteland. Was he being watched? Would the Russians open fire from their hiding places the moment he revealed himself? Were they closing behind him, like hunters herding their prey onto the waiting guns?

The thought almost made McQuade double back along the wall to search for a new route. But he knew he had no time.

The sound of automatic gunfire seemed to be coming closer, and closing from every direction.

He set himself and took a last deep breath. He could feel his nerves jangling and his muscles had drawn taut, as though anticipating the heavy slog of the first bullet.

He was just about to spring from cover when a flash of movement caught the corner of his eye. He jerked his head around and ducked down at the same time. He saw a dirty square patch of cloth, being waved from the darkened doorway of a building to his right. McQuade stared hard as a fresh wave of doubts and alarm assailed him.

For several seconds the white cloth waved, and then a shadowy figure stepped into the doorway. He looked like a middle-aged man, dressed in a grimy, stained suit. His face was pale, his clothes rumpled. He fluttered the flag again and then beckoned McQuade to him with an urgent wave of his arm.

"Fuck!" McQuade felt a sharp stab of panic and confusion. He let out a long breath. Sweat trickled down his brow and into his eyes.

He looked out across the open ground to the far row of ruined buildings and then back to the shadowed doorway. The man still stood there, vague and ill-defined in the gloom. He waved the white cloth again.

"Fuck!"

A gunshot decided the matter. The sound of the rifle was a startlingly loud *'crack!'* in the tense fraught silence. McQuade never saw the round strike but the sound of it echoed across the empty space. It sounded close, from somewhere behind him. He flinched involuntarily.

"Fuck!"

Running doubled over, drenched in a lather of sweat and cringing with fear, McQuade dodged around the ruins of a gutted car and angled right, towards the shadowed doorway. His heart was pounding in his chest, his breathing loud and rasping in his ears. He reached the opening and flung himself inside, throwing up the Beretta even as he crashed to the ground and rolled onto his back.

"Don't move!" he shouted. "Don't move a fucking muscle or I'll fire!"

*

The man stood quite still and lifted his hands into the air. McQuade scrambled onto his knees, the barrel of the Beretta pointed at the stranger's chest.

The man was large and heavily set. He looked close to sixty and he wore a dark suit, holed and frayed at the elbows. His clothes were rumpled, his iron-grey hair disheveled. His skin hung in loose folds beneath his eyes and from his jowls, giving him the amiable appearance of a butcher, or perhaps a plumber. But his gaze was bright and calm and intelligent.

McQuade scrambled to his knees and kept the barrel of the Beretta aimed squarely at the stranger's chest.

"Who are you?"

The man opened his mouth to answer, but another stray rifle shot split the fraught silence. McQuade ducked and flinched instinctively, though the wicked retort of the bullet sounded far away and slightly muffled.

The middle-aged man peered warily around the frame of the open door and looked out across the desolated wasteland, ignoring the gun McQuade held aimed at him. He stayed very still for several seconds, his eyes searching for danger, and then ducked back into the gloomy shadow of the ruined building.

He waved his arm for McQuade to follow then went shuffling down a dark corridor littered with debris and rubble.

For another long moment McQuade hesitated. He licked his lips and cast a final glance out through the doorway into the daylight.

The stranger reached the end of the passage and stood, waiting for McQuade. The pilot still hesitated. The man waved his arm again and disappeared into dark shadow.

"Fuck!"

McQuade followed.

The man stood waiting for him by another internal doorway. The building's roof had partially collapsed. Wires dangled from the shattered ceiling and drifting dust hung like smoke in the air. The man took McQuade's arm and steered him through a jungle of debris. Bodies, mostly still, lay buried amidst the rubble. McQuade saw a young child's arm protruding from a heaped mound of debris. It was grey with a powder of ash, the fingers stiffened into a claw.

Shattered glass crunched under his feet and the walls around them seemed to groan as if close to collapse.

They passed down a narrow passage, heading towards another door. Through a shattered window McQuade looked out across an alley to see a building on the far side of the street collapse, sending up a billowing cloud of dust and smoke. An explosion somewhere close by shook the ground beneath their feet and threw them staggering against a wall. Coughing and choking, the two men stumbled on.

The man heaved open the door at the end of the passage and McQuade saw they were standing in a narrow back alley that led to a courtyard beneath a nearby building. The path was partially blocked by an overturned car, the rubber tires melted, the chassis burned black. There was a body inside the vehicle, one charred arm thrust through a shattered window.

"Where are you taking me?" McQuade asked.

The man said nothing. Still clinging to McQuade's arm the two of them dashed along the alley and then plunged into the shadows of the courtyard.

"What is your name?"

The man skirted a mound of collapsed bricks and ran through a drifting mist of smoke. They emerged at a dead end. A sudden hot flush of blind panic overwhelmed McQuade. The hairs along his forearms and at the back of his neck bristled and itched with sweaty dread. He felt like a hunted animal that had been led, blundering, into a deadly trap. He turned frantically to search for an escape. The man seized his arm tightly and pointed.

Set into the rubble-strewn concrete pavement was an old wooden trapdoor with an iron ring, obscured by broken wooden beams, slabs of concrete and shattered roof tiles. The man bent to the debris and began to carefully set it aside.

"Where are we going?" McQuade's tone was edged with rising alarm.

The man cleared the trapdoor and heaved it open. He pointed down into the yawning darkness, then stepped back. McQuade saw now that the debris over the trapdoor had been carefully arranged to camouflage the opening. He peered down. A set of old stone steps descended in gloomy darkness. He guessed it was a cellar or a basement. He could smell the faint odors of smoke and of stale cooking. The man pushed McQuade and gestured impatiently, his head turning quickly to check over his shoulder for signs of pursuit.

McQuade went down the dark steps, wielding the Beretta warily, like a condemned prisoner on his way to the gallows.

*

The air was cool and clammy at the bottom of the steps. McQuade stood like a blind man, groping for something solid to orientate himself. The blackness was absolute, yet in the stillness he sensed some unseen presence.

The man pulled the trapdoor shut and followed him down the steps, moving more assuredly. He felt for McQuade's arm, gripped it, and then fumbled into his pocket for a cigarette lighter. The small flickering flame lit the tunnel.

It was a passage made of rough-hewn stone, wide enough for them to walk side by side. It only stretched for ten yards, their footsteps echoing hollowly off the arched walls before it ended in yet another door. McQuade heard a soft scuffle of muffled movement from somewhere ahead of him and froze. The man rapped three times on the door, then McQuade heard a bolt being shot. The door opened from the inside and a gentle glow of yellow light filled the open space.

McQuade stepped into a large underground space, lit by a dozen flickering candles. The air was damp and where the light reflected against the walls it showed the raw stone walls stained with centuries of soot and grime.

Huddled on the cellar floor with their backs to the walls sat over a dozen men, women and children. The closest woman's clothes were torn and smeared with dirt. She looked to be aged in her thirties, but her expression was so harrowed, so haunted, that McQuade was unsure. Her hair was matted, her face so pale and her skin so waxen that she might have been dead. She lifted her eyes to McQuade and they were filled with anguish and desolation. Beside her a young child sat sobbing and next to the child crouched an elderly man with a snowy-white cap of hair. He was clinging to the hand of a young teenage girl whose face was smeared with blood and dirt, her eyes wide and staring. The girl turned her head slowly towards McQuade and a flicker of life registered in her eyes.

There were other refugees sitting in the shadows; McQuade saw two young uniformed soldiers, brandishing weapons, and there were more bedraggled men and women in the far corner of the cellar, huddled around a small gas stove.

He turned back to face the middle-aged man and reached into a pocket of his flight suit.

"Here," he held out a small piece of paper. The man unfolded the page and lifted it up to the flickering glow of his cigarette lighter.

The blood chit had a picture of the American flag and an inscription that read:

I am an American and do not speak your language. I will not harm you! I bear no malice towards your people. My friend, please provide me with food, water, shelter, clothing and necessary medical attention. Also, please provide safe passage to the nearest friendly forces of any country supporting the Americans and their allies. You will be rewarded for assisting me when you present the number and my name to the American authorities.

The message was printed in five languages, including Ukrainian, Polish and German, and had numbers on each corner that could be torn off and redeemed for a monetary reward.

The man studied the page carefully and nodded. He stared at McQuade for a moment longer, his pale eyes were direct and disturbing – the eyes of a prophet or a crusader – and then he handed the card back to McQuade.

"You understand?" McQuade prompted. "I am an American pilot. My name is Lieutenant Steven McQuade. I am fighting in Ukraine against the Russians. My fighter jet was shot down, and I need your help to return to the Allied lines. If there are Ukraine army units nearby, please take me to them and you will be rewarded by my government."

The man nodded again, then abruptly held out his hand. "My name is Maksim Guslistaya. It's a pleasure to meet you. We will certainly do everything in our power to reunite you with your American Air Force colleagues," he said in perfect English.

*

"You speak English?" McQuade felt a rush of irrational anger. "Then why the hell didn't you answer my questions?"

The man shrugged and said elusively, ignoring the protest in McQuade's voice, "Sometimes talking is good, and sometimes it is bad. You did not ask your questions at a time where I could engage in idle chatter."

The man loosened the knot of his tie, dipped it in a bucket of water, and used the cloth to gently wipe the face of a young child lying on the stone floor beside them. He watched pensively as McQuade scooped a handful of warm potato stew from out of a tin plate and ate.

"Do you think," Maksim asked in a quiet voice, "that the Russians saw you eject from your fighter jet?"

"I can't see how they could miss it," McQuade said bitterly. "They certainly would have seen my plane crash. I can't imagine they didn't see my parachute as well."

"Then they will be hunting you."

"Yes."

"Then they will be close," the man said and gnawed thoughtfully at his lip. "They will have patrols out across the entire precinct searching for you."

"Yes."

The man made a pained face. McQuade became suspicious. "Are you worried for your own safety, and your people?"

"Of course," Maksim admitted. "You are not the only one fleeing from the Russian Army, Lieutenant. Look around you; look at the faces of these people. They are innocent victims. They are refugees of a terrible war that they want no part in."

McQuade raised an eyebrow and gestured at the two young uniformed soldiers in the far corner of the room. "They're not civilians."

"No," the man nodded. "They are guards."

"Guards?" McQuade asked. "Yours? Are they protecting you?"

"Yes and no…"

"Are you someone important? Maybe the Russians want you more than they want me."

"I am sure of it," the man smiled thinly.

"So, you are important."

"I am a university history professor, Lieutenant McQuade. Before war broke out across Europe, I was lecturing modern history at Borys Grinchenko Kyiv University and living a humble life with my wife in our small apartment," he said it with simple pride. "Are you not a student of history, Lieutenant?"

"No."

Maksim looked disappointed, as though McQuade had somehow slipped in his estimation. "There is no greater teacher than the lessons we can learn from our past. A people without the knowledge of their past history, origin and culture is like a tree without roots. Marcus Garvey said that. Do you know of him?"

"No."

The Ukrainian disguised his surprise at McQuade's ignorance. "He was a Jamaican political activist who died during the years of the Second World War." For a moment it looked like the man would say more, but he politely changed the subject, looking around instead at the gloomy cellar and the faces of the refugees before he spoke again.

"So, what does your American pilot training tell you to do when you are shot down, Lieutenant?"

"We are taught to escape and evade the enemy," McQuade answered.

"On your own?"

McQuade ignored the hint of scorn in the man's voice which suggested the American would already have blundered into a Russian patrol and been captured if the man had not found him first.

"If necessary."

"But it's easier if you have the cooperation of willing civilians, yes? Otherwise, why would you hand me the paper you did?" The Ukrainian smiled a cunning smile of understanding. "You need help, I think." Instead of waiting for an answer he picked up his own plate of watery stew and began to eat carefully. There was not much food to spare so he ate just a little then handed the leftovers to the hungry child sitting beside him.

"I got shot down flying a close air support mission, trying to help your soldiers who were under attack," McQuade let the edge of resentment in his voice flash like a drawn dagger's blade as he rose to his feet. "You talk about me needing the cooperation of civilians?" he stabbed an accusing finger down at the man. "Well yes, it's true… just like your Army needs American support."

Maksim stared at McQuade with his eyes narrowed. He showed no offense. He looked like he was carefully appraising the young pilot. McQuade's face was flushed, his temper simmering. He knew his chances of surviving even a few hours in the ruins of Kiev without the help of the civilian population were practically zero. Yet at the same time he had no desire to humiliate or debase himself for that help.

The man seemed to read his mind. "It is a long journey to the front lines, Lieutenant… But there is another alternative. You could come with us."

"With you? Where?"

"We are traveling south a few miles. There is a place we must reach. Once we get there, we could gladly escort you to the battlefront, so you can be returned to your Air Force."

"And if I refuse?"

"Why would you?" the man asked reasonably, but there was a veiled mocking challenge in his voice. "Your route will still return you safely to your comrades. Only it will be a little more circuitous and perhaps a little less dangerous."

"Traveling with a handful of refugee women and children?"

"God willing, the Russians will not find us, but we will pray before we leave to be sure the Lord will protect our steps."

McQuade could not conceal his astonishment. "That's your plan? To pray to God?" the pilot was appalled.

A child on the far side of the room began crying. A woman leaped to her feet to quickly soothe the girl. Everyone in the cellar seemed to cringe at the loud and sudden noise. Instinctively they cast their eyes to the ceiling and cowered as though expecting to hear the sudden roar of automatic gunfire, or the alerted voices of Russian soldiers. For a long moment everyone seemed to hold their breath.

"So, you do not believe in history or God," the bitterness of Maksim's accusation surprised McQuade.

"God is irrelevant to me," McQuade defended himself. "He's had nothing to do with my life."

"Nothing to do with your life?" the man looked aghast.

"Nothing."

"Maybe you are just not aware of the influence He has had!" Maksim said with sudden passion. "Without God, life is meaningless."

"Maybe for you," McQuade swatted the claim away with a dismissive shrug. He felt unaccountably tired. Every muscle in his body ached. He felt his eyes droop, and he had to fight to stay alert.

McQuade distracted himself by sweeping a glance around the cellar. In the far corner sat a woman, staring brazenly at him. She looked to be aged in her twenties. Despite her bedraggled appearance she had a proud, defiant lift to her chin. She glared at McQuade with cold taunting eyes until he looked away.

The Ukrainian man cleared his throat and reached into his coat pocket for a cigarette. The pungent aroma of tobacco filled the small space and a thin feather of blue haze drifted across the low ceiling.

"We are leaving here when darkness falls, Lieutenant, and we are heading south until we reach our destination. You can come with us, or you can attempt to survive in the ruins of the city alone."

McQuade sighed his abdication. "I'll come."

"Good," Maksim said and smiled for the first time. "Between now and then you should rest and sleep," his tone took a sarcastic twist. "I hope our prayers for God's guidance do not disturb you…"

Chapter 4:

The refugees gathered at the foot of the stone steps an hour after nightfall and listened to Maksim explain their route. It was foolish, he said, to try to reach their destination in one night. To attempt to travel so far with Russian patrols criss-crossing the streets and snipers amongst the city's ruins would be inviting disaster. Instead, they must be patient. Their first task was to reach the factory buildings on Vasyl Potkrya Avenue. There, amongst the ruins, they would find a new place to hide until it was safe to continue their journey. But to reach the factory complex, they must traverse a highway that would be patrolled by Russian sentries, and skirt a complex of apartment blocks. McQuade watched the refugees faces lit by the small light of the candles and saw the rapt admiration and esteem with which they regarded the man. They listened in silence, nodded their willing comprehension, and roused themselves for the dangers they would face. After the explanations in English, Maksim slipped into Ukrainian and addressed the group again. This time there were scowls, and an elderly woman at the edges of the group spoke quickly. Maksim held up his hands and nodded.

People rolled their meagre belongings up into blankets and checked their weapons. Mothers swaddled their babies and strapped them to their bodies. The two young uniformed soldiers carried AK-74s, but most of the other men in the group were armed with old bolt-action rifles. A couple of the women carried hand grenades and pistols.

The man had told them there might be fighting; the highway, he said, was heavily patrolled by Russian soldiers and armored vehicles. If they were caught in the open, they must be prepared to fight their way to freedom.

McQuade checked his Beretta and listened to the Ukrainian's easy manner as he spoke. He was calm and confident with a charismatic presence that people were drawn to.

When everyone was ready Maksim went quietly to the top of the steps and put his shoulder to the trap door. It opened without a sound, and a wash of cold fresh air spilled into the cellar. He eased his head through the opening like a submarine commander at the periscope and turned in a slow circle. Satisfied, he ducked back down into the gloom and waved his arm urgently.

The two uniformed soldiers went first, creeping stealthily up the steps, their weapons ready. McQuade noticed for the first time that one of the men had a small steel case handcuffed to his wrist. The container was about a foot long and high, but just a few inches thick. It was sealed with a padlock and smeared with dirt and mud to dull the metallic shine. The soldier tucked the case inside his uniform jacket as he went up the steps, leaving just the links of chain to his wrist dangling loosely so he would be free to wield his weapon.

"What's that soldier carrying?" McQuade asked Maksim when it was his turn at last to clamber up through the cellar door.

"Documents for safe keeping," the Ukrainian said casually. It was not an answer to satisfy McQuade's curiosity; it was an answer to dissuade further questions. McQuade asked none.

He was about to climb the last few steps when the man snatched at his arm to hold him back. He leaned his face close to McQuade's so the words were just a whisper. "Nobody trusts you, American, so do nothing to bring attention to yourself. These people have survived on their wits for days in this wasteland. Do nothing reckless that will endanger them – or I will shoot you myself."

Through the cellar door, McQuade emerged with his Beretta drawn into a cold night. A chill, fitful wind swirled through the bomb-ravaged ruins, kicking up dust and driving lingering smoke across the sky. The two uniformed soldiers were standing in deep shadow twenty yards further along the alley. One of the men showed himself and waved McQuade forward. He went quietly. The rest of the group were hidden from view behind the cover of a brick wall. Several of the women had wrapped their faces in strips of dirty rag to cover their mouths and noses from the dust and smoke.

Maksim was the last one to emerge from the cellar. He closed the trapdoor carefully behind him and strode purposefully to where the soldiers stood guard.

"No dangers?"

"No," a soldier muttered.

He waved the refugees forward and they fell into a straggling column, like ducklings behind a mother duck. The man led the way with the two soldiers at his side. McQuade drifted back until he was in the center of the column, trudging in the darkness through the devastated cityscape.

At midnight they found the abandoned ruins of a gas station and Maksim allowed them to rest briefly. The walls of the building still stood, but the ceiling had collapsed in upon itself. Some of the women foraged through overturned shelves of tinned goods and loaves of stale bread. The building had been partially engulfed in fire; the gas bowsers outside the shattered glass doors were blackened and melted. Amongst the rubble outside the building were the dark mounds of unburied corpses.

"So far we have been lucky," Maksim said and turned to knock three times on a charred beam of wood.

McQuade looked mystified. The man saw the puzzlement in the pilot's face.

"It is traditional for Ukrainians to knock three times on wood to ward off the evil eye, Lieutenant. I do it to ensure our continued good fortune."

"The evil eye?" McQuade could not conceal his astonishment.

"Of course," Maksim was entirely serious. "Knocking on wood wards off the magic of ill-intended people. A hateful glance can summon great misfortune unless we protect ourselves."

McQuade was incredulous. "You're making a joke at my expense, right?"

"Absolutely not," Maksim said. "The superstition was inherited from our ancestors. We Ukrainians are very superstitious people. In ancient times people believed that if you touched a wooden surface, you also touched the Christ, who was crucified on a wooden cross. To knock on wood is to ask for holy protection."

"And why three times? Why not four, or eight?" McQuade mocked.

Maksim's face darkened and his tone became surly. "Because three is a sacred number for Christians. You would know that, Lieutenant, if you were one of God's children."

They lapsed into another tense silence. McQuade felt churlish for mocking the other man's beliefs.

"Is your wife amongst the women traveling with us?" he offered the olive branch after a long pause.

"No," Maksim snapped, then admonished himself for answering in such a harsh voice. He offered McQuade a rueful shrug of apology, and his tone softened with emotion.

"My wife died on the first day of the ground war," he said. "She had been visiting her sister in Luhansk – it is a city in eastern Ukraine, near the border with Russia in the disputed Donbass region. She was killed by Russian infantry when they attacked."

McQuade was unsure how to respond. "I'm sorry for your loss," he said clumsily.

The man shrugged his shoulders and his expression turned grief-stricken. "That was the moment I vowed to do all I could to rid this country of our oppressors," Maksim said. "Her death gives me the strength every day to go on fighting."

They rested for fifteen minutes and then moved on again into the night. McQuade watched the soldier with the small metal box tucked down inside his uniform jacket. Every few minutes he touched at his chest, as if to reassure himself that the steel container was still safe. The chain dangling from his wrist made soft rattling noises as he swung his weapon from side to side, traversing the area ahead of their advance.

They reached the verge of the highway in the bleak early hours of the morning. The wind had strengthened and swung around to the north. The air turned bitterly cold and then it began to rain; a soft pearly mist that diffused everything into a bleary haze and turned the dust and bomb-churned ground to mud.

Maksim ordered the refugees to remain hidden amidst the shadows of a clump of fire-ravaged trees and scouted forward at a crouch until he found a stretch of highway close to a bend and bordered on both sides by high mounds of rubble.

"We will cross here," he decided.

The dark was eerily still, but in the distance, carried on the wind, they could hear far-away artillery fire and the muted rumble of vehicle engines. Even in the dead of night, the fight for Ukraine went on.

The first man across the highway was one of the uniformed soldiers. He ran at a doubled-over sprint, moving like a flitting wraith. He crossed the blacktop unseen and dropped into shadow. The refugees followed in singles and pairs while those on either side of the road held their breath, tense and anxious.

McQuade felt a hand on his shoulder and Maksim whispered in his ear. "You go next."

He rose to his haunches and looked right, then left. The highway was dark and deserted, the bitumen slick and shiny from the recent rain. He tucked his Beretta inside his shoulder holster and crept to the verge of the highway. A figure crawled close to him. It was the same young woman who had challenged him with her glare in the cellar. McQuade felt the hard resilience of the woman's thigh through her threadbare skirt, pressed against his own leg, and heard the urgent rasp of her breathing.

McQuade checked the highway again and saw soft wavering yellow light somewhere in the distance. The light was diffused and seemed to float below the rim of the skyline. He sprang to his feet and started to run. The woman at his side ran with him.

They reached the center of the highway and McQuade realized the wavering lights were the headlights of an approaching Russian APC. He could hear the sudden growl of the engine changing gears as it approached an incline. In a few seconds it would crest the rise, and they would be stranded in the middle of the road. He snatched the woman's hand and flung her ahead of him, planting his palm in the small of her back and shoving her with all his strength. She went staggering across the tarmac, her arms flailing, and fell in a heap on the far side of the road. McQuade dived after her and the two of them crashed together in the wet grass. The woman lay beneath him in the muddy ground. McQuade clamped a hand over her gasping mouth.

He lifted his head and saw the dark ominous shape of a Russian eight-wheeled armored troop carrier cruising along the center of the highway, its turret traversing slowly from side to side. McQuade ducked his head down as the vehicle's lights passed over where they lay hidden. He could feel his heart beating and the woman squirming and struggling beneath him. He tried to still her with a blazing glare of his eyes.

Then suddenly the Russian vehicle stopped, and McQuade heard the rear door of the troop carrier swung down. The woman beneath him went very still. McQuade could see the fear in her eyes.

A Russian soldier's voice called out in the night, and the reply was a hiss of static from the vehicle's radio. The man spoke again then took a few steps towards the edge of the highway. McQuade could hear the scrape of the man's muddy boots as he drew closer.

Another voice from further away called out, the words drowned out by the rumble of the vehicle's idling engine. McQuade lifted his head with infinite slowness until he could see.

A Russian soldier stood ten feet away on the shoulder of the road, peering into the black night towards where they hid. McQuade held his breath. The rain grew stronger, then became a downpour. It hammered against McQuade's back and swept across the highway in grey curtains. A new voice, imperative and guttural, spoke a harsh command and the Russian soldier obediently turned on his heel and ran splashing back to the APC.

McQuade let himself breathe. "They're going," he whispered.

The sound of the APC rose and the vehicle moved off, belching black diesel exhaust into the night.

The rest of the refugees crossed the highway without incident. Maksim and the uniformed soldier protecting the steel box were the last to cross.

Together the straggle of refugees moved off through a narrow maze of buildings that looked to McQuade to have once been a complex of small apartments. Many of the buildings had been hit by artillery shells; the entire city block flattened to ugly ruins of fire scorched rubble.

Maksim called another halt and went forward alone into the night. When he returned a few minutes later, he was drenched and breathing hard.

"We have come too far east," he announced somberly. "Vasyl Potkrya Avenue is that way," he pointed. "But I have scouted as far ahead as the next intersection. If we move out now and travel quickly, we can still reach the factory buildings before dawn. The enemy are nowhere to be seen."

At which point, from behind a line of bomb-damaged ruins on the far side of the road, the Russians opened fire.

*

McQuade saw Maksim dive to his right and he threw himself sideways. He landed on a pile of broken bricks by the front door of a bomb-ravaged apartment. His teeth slammed together and his mouth filled with blood, then the Beretta was in his hand and he was aiming and firing into the night. A Russian bullet ricocheted off a buckled sheet of corrugated iron, another cracked into the cement-rendered wall just inches above his head. From somewhere in the shadows nearby he heard a woman wail in excruciating pain.

McQuade, shaken by the shock of being shot at, struggled to make sense of the sudden riot of chaotic noise and confusion. He tried to estimate the size of the enemy force by the volume of their fire. They had automatic weapons and they were shooting from behind a darkly silhouetted line of rubble about a hundred yards away. He saw the bright winking lights of their muzzle flashes and guessed it was no more than a handful of infantry – probably a Russian patrol that had stumbled upon them by sheer accident.

McQuade crawled forward through the rubble. A bullet tore a chunk out of the cement wall a few inches from his head. Backlit against the soft glow of distant fires he could make out the shapes of several Russian soldiers. One was kneeling beside a collapsed chimney firing across a courtyard. The others were all laying prone atop a massive heap of collapsed wreckage and roofing iron, shooting down on them from a slight elevation. He sensed there were other Russians on that rise of debris too, using their height advantage to pin the refugees down.

The Ukrainians had scattered. Most of the women scrambled into the small cover of nearby bomb-ravaged buildings. The men threw up their weapons and returned panicked fire. The two uniformed soldiers in the group had moved with the instincts and understanding of trained infantrymen. They were both behind solid cover, and both firing short controlled bursts up into the debris where the Russians were concealed.

McQuade crawled past the two soldiers on his stomach, saw an elderly man lying on his back in a spreading pool of blood, and then cautiously raised his head above a chunk of twisted steel to orientate himself. A rifle cracked to his right. Another man screamed out in pain and sagged forward, clutching at his chest. His weapon clattered to the ground and he fell to his knees.

McQuade saw Maksim off to his left. He had an ancient bolt-action rifle at his shoulder, firing from one knee into the darkness.

"Maksim, if we stay here, we're all dead," McQuade reached the man and hissed at him.

The man fired again, the crack of the rifle obscenely loud in the night, then worked the bolt of the weapon with unpracticed hands to reload.

"If we make a run for it they will hunt us down like dogs," Maksim snarled. "We have to kill them."

"Well this isn't the way to do it!" McQuade had to shout over the sound of the man firing again. In a fit of frustration, McQuade peered across the dark void through a gap in the rubble and studied the Russian position more closely. He felt certain the refugees were being pinned down by just a handful of enemy. But the longer the desultory firefight continued, the more likely it was that other Russians would be drawn to the sounds of combat. If the refugees were to escape into the night and evade pursuit, the Russians had to be silenced – permanently and quickly.

He went back to where Maksim knelt and grabbed at his arm, dragging him down behind cover. McQuade leaned close.

"There is a stretch of dead ground further to the right of our position," he explained quickly, checking the Beretta in his hand for ammunition as he spoke. "I think I can disappear into the shadows and circle around behind the Russians. Can you keep them distracted?"

Maksim narrowed his eyes and studied the American pilot carefully. "Yes."

McQuade knew that to stay where they were and to engage in a protracted firefight with Russian infantry was to die. The Russians weren't trying to rush their position. They wanted to pin the refugees down until support troops arrived. Perhaps radio messages had already been exchanged.

The only way, McQuade knew, was to carry the attack to the Russians; a suicidal charge that would take the enemy by surprise in their rear. He realized he might be killed in the attempt. But he would surely die if he did nothing.

He heard Maksim bark a string of orders in Ukrainian and then the refugees scattered through the rubble began firing in earnest. Two young women ran forward from out of the shadows and picked up fallen weapons, adding to the concentrated fusillade. The Russian soldier firing from the shadows of the collapsed chimney was flung backwards, shot in the throat. He crumpled to the ground choking on his blood.

McQuade took a last deep breath and dashed to his right, running doubled-over until he reached the depression and could hurl himself head-first into the dense black shadows of dead ground. He found himself lying amidst a series of overlapping bomb craters, the bottoms filled with small dark pools of stagnant, stinking water. He scrambled over the muddy earth and reached the far embankment. Cautiously he peered above the rim of the depression. The rubble mound where the Russians were firing from was twenty paces to his left. He could make out indistinct shapes moving on its crest. The muzzle flashes from each spurt of automatic fire leaped from the Russian weapons like dragon-breaths of flame.

McQuade waited for the exhilaration of battle to grip him as it did when he was in the cockpit of his Viper; the rush of adrenalin, the macabre fatalistic sense of the inevitable – but it did not come. Instead, he sprang to his feet with fear churning in his guts.

Above McQuade, crouched on the crest of the rubble mound, the Russian Corporal commanding the five-man patrol ordered his troops to concentrate their aim on the maze of bomb-ravaged buildings a hundred yards to their front.

McQuade stealthily circled the rubble mound, and as he moved in the shadows the rifle cracks of the refugees still firing echoed across the darkness. He was gambling on his instincts that the Russians were just a small patrol. He skirted further around the foot of the mound until he saw an incline of fallen rocks. He started to scramble up the rock pile, clawing at the loose rubble with his hands. He heard the Russians fire again; they were shooting from directly above where he was crouched, with their backs to him. He gritted his teeth and forced himself to move quickly, the sounds of his ascent smothered by the deafening staccato of the enemy's machine guns. Fear was huge inside him. His guts turned sour and leaden with terror.

He reached out for a protruding iron pipe to hoist himself upwards. The rod was about three feet long, bent slightly at one end. He pulled it from the ground as he climbed. His legs began to ache with the strain, his hands were cut and bleeding in a dozen places. His knees felt bruised and his lungs burned, but the rage and the fear came upon him. He crested the rubble mount, panting and gasping. His only conscious thought was to kill.

He wielded the iron pipe like a two-handed sword, screaming an incoherent cry of terror and anger. He saw a Russian soldier turn towards him. The man's face had been blackened by camouflage paint, but his eyes showed wide and white, and his mouth hung open like a deep dark pit of gaping surprise. McQuade swung the pipe with all his strength and struck the soldier in the side of the head. He heard bone crack and then felt the man's skull crush. The flesh under the weighty crude weapon turned soft and rubbery. The Russian felt backwards and another man rose in his place, swinging his machine gun round to fire and roaring a challenge. Suddenly the pent-up terror churning within McQuade vented itself. He took two lunging steps forward over the loose ground and swung the iron pipe again. The steel struck the man in the ribs and he seemed to fold forward and wrap himself around the blow, the air punched from his lungs in a groan of muffled agony. McQuade tried to free the pipe but as the Russian fell, he wrenched the weapon loose of McQuade's grip. The pilot thrust his hand into his flying suit and pulled the Beretta from its holster. A flurry of shots blazed past his ear, the passage of the bullets so close that they scorched the flesh of his cheek. He fired back into the darkened chaos and shot his attacker in the chest from point blank range. The Russian tumbled backwards and went rolling, already dead, down the rubble slope. Another Russian swung his machine gun like an axe and the steel stock caught McQuade on the knee. He howled in agony and bared his teeth like a wild animal. He snarled at the

Russian and lunged for him, sending the man tumbling backwards with McQuade's weight on top of him. The Russian cried out in alarm and cracked the back of his skull on a slab of concrete. McQuade wrapped his hands around the stunned man's throat and began to choke the life out of him. He heard another shot whistle close by in the night and then a rustle of running movement and splashing boots. He snarled at the man beneath him, crushing down and squeezing with all his strength until the enemy soldier suddenly stopped resisting and went very still.

McQuade rolled off the body, gasping, his chest heaving. He was spattered in mud and blood. His hands shook uncontrollably.

When he looked up, his eyes were still unfocussed and red with the mist of his rage. Several of the refugees had reached the crest of the rubble pile. They were rummaging through the pockets of the dead Russians, searching for food and spare ammunition. Maksim stood over McQuade with a curious expression on his face. He extended his hand and lifted the Viper pilot unsteadily to his feet.

"Okay," the Ukrainian professor conceded. "So now you have proven yourself worthy of our trust, American," he said grimly. "But this is no place and no time for respite. We must gather up our wounded and get away from here quickly. The rest of the Russian Army cannot be far away."

Chapter 5:

The refugees reached the factory buildings on Vasyl Potkrya Avenue an hour before dawn, their nerves frayed, their bodies strained past the point of exhaustion. Maksim led them to the vast shell of a tractor factory and forced open a side door covered with red warning labels and Ukrainian language safety signs.

The factory – like every other building on the Vasyl Potkrya industrial estate – had been bombed by Russian aircraft and shelled by artillery during the first days of the war. The corrugated iron roof, suspended a hundred feet above their head on a frame of steel gantries, had partially collapsed, and the western end of the building was blackened by soot and ash.

The interior of the factory was cavernous and gloomy. Through the gaping hole in the roof glowed the first pale hint of morning but at ground level the factory floor remained eerily dark and deeply shadowed. McQuade peered cautiously into the gloom. Above the centerline of the building's concrete floor he could see a framework of steel girders from which were suspended cranes on pulleys that overhung an assembly line. Several farm tractors were in the process of being constructed. In the maze of steel beams overhead, flocks of pigeons flapped their wings. The air was cold and still.

"There is a basement level at the east end," Maksim said, explaining that his wife's cousin once worked at the factory. He led them through a maze of office cubicles and then along a corridor lined on each side with cardboard boxes of machinery parts. At the end of the passage was a set of steel steps and a handrail that descended. Maksim went first, holding his cigarette lighter in front of him to illuminate the way.

The basement level was divided into a network of tunnel-like passageways that criss-crossed beneath the main factory floor and had been used by workers for staff lunchrooms, shower blocks and for storage. The walls were bare concrete and brick, the ceilings so low that McQuade had to stoop. The air in the subterranean passages smelled of stale sweat and cigarette smoke.

"We will be safe here for the day," Maksim declared. Candles were lit and the refugees wrapped themselves in their blankets and collapsed, exhausted, on the bare concrete floor.

McQuade went a few yards further along the dark passage and sat with a weary sigh. Fatigue and physical exhaustion assailed him in waves. His eyes felt filled with grit. He scraped the palm of his hand across his jaw and the unshaven stubble there crackled like electricity.

Over his shoulder he watched Maksim surreptitiously. The Ukrainian was talking quietly to the uniformed soldier who wore the mysterious steel case handcuffed to his wrist. They exchanged a few muttered words and then the soldier reached into his boot and produced a key to unlock the cuffs. He handed the steel case and the key to Maksim, then picked up his weapon and went striding back down the tunnel towards the stairs.

Maksim fastened the cuff to his wrist and then looked up with an expression akin to guilt on his face. He saw McQuade watching him. He stiffened and thrust out his jaw. McQuade closed his eyes and let his head sag back against the cold concrete wall. He was asleep in moments.

A shuffle of commotion and a mutter of voices roused him. He had no idea how long he had slept. He blinked owlishly and rubbed his red-rimmed eyes. Every muscle in his body had seized stiff. He groaned and tried to arch his back. The refugees were gathered in a group by the foot of the steps. McQuade came to his feet like an arthritic old man and took a few wincing steps.

"Are you hungry, American?" Maksim stood head and shoulders above the refugees gathered around him. "Come. Eat."

Against the far wall of the tunnel stood four corner stacks of bricks supporting a buckled piece of iron. Beneath the metal hotplate, the refugees had built a small fire from foraged timber that lay strewn across the bombed factory floor. A drift of grey smoke crawled up the wall and hung close to the ceiling.

The gathered refugees parted just enough to allow McQuade to see the hands of the uniformed soldier. He was carrying an armful of meaty steaks, the blood dripping through his fingers. He handed the cuts of meat to a woman who dexterously ripped away the pelt and placed each one on the hotplate. The meat hissed and sizzled juices.

"Horse steaks," Maksim explained to McQuade. "Oleksandr found a dead animal by the side of the road. It had been killed by artillery fragments," he acknowledged the uniformed soldier.

"Horse?"

Maksim looked puzzled. "Yes, of course. Have you never eaten horse flesh before, American?"

"No."

"Then you have never been truly hungry," Maksim said. A woman dropped to her knees and began to feed twigs and sticks into the flames. After a few minutes she picked up the slabs of cooked meat in her fingers and turned them over. The smells of cooking drifted down the tunnel.

"Horse flesh varies in color. Meat from younger horses is usually lighter in color and flavor, while the meat cut from older horses has a deeper color and flavor. Personally, I prefer older horse flesh," Maksim gave his opinion. "Horses have a lot of muscle, so you would think their meat is a lot tougher than beef steak. Not so! Cooked just right, horse flesh is very tender…"

When the steaks were cooked, the refugees sat in small groups and ate with their fingers, gnawing at the meat ravenously. Many had not eaten properly in days. Maksim handed the steel case back to Oleksandr and the young soldier re-attached the handcuff to his wrist.

"You look like you have much on your mind, American," Maksim clamped his hand on McQuade's shoulder and tactfully lead him away from the rest of the group. They walked along the gloomy tunnel until they were well out of earshot. It was almost pitch black. The maze of subterranean passageways seemed to run for miles.

"I have questions," McQuade said flatly.

Maksim made an untroubled face. "Then ask."

"What are you hiding in that steel case? Have you stolen money? Is that why you're fleeing south?"

"You think I'm a common criminal?" Maksim's tone registered his offense. It was too dark in the tunnel to read his expression.

"I think it would explain a great deal," McQuade avoided making a direct accusation.

Maksim fell silent for a long moment. When he spoke, his words seemed to come out of the blackness like the haunting undulation of a ghost.

"There is no money in the case, Lieutenant."

"Well it's not documents. No one guards paperwork in a steel case at the end of a pair of handcuffs."

"You are right, Lieutenant. There is no paperwork in the case," Maksim sighed like he was growing bored with the American's questions.

"Then what are you hiding? And what makes it so precious that it's being carried under the escort of two Ukrainian Army soldiers?"

"It's none of your concern, American."

"It is," McQuade countered. "I might get killed because of it. In fact, I think the only reason you helped me escape the Russians is because it gave you another man and another gun to help ensure you reach your objective. You didn't help me out of the goodness of your heart. You did it for your own selfish purposes."

"My own selfish purposes?" the rage came into Maksim's voice like a sudden crack of thunder. "You ignorant, arrogant young fool. You know nothing of history, nothing of God, and nothing of the world. How dare you accuse me…" his voice trailed off, the bluster of his temper blown away as quickly as it had arrived. Maksim drew a deep breath and McQuade could hear him pacing the ground, though in the inky blackness he could see nothing of the other man.

For a long moment there was only the soft footfalls of the Ukrainian's steps and the sound of ragged breathing. Then, in the distance, another sound filled the void. It was the muted rumble of war; the sound of Russian artillery shells made faint and indistinct by distance and the barrier of thick concrete walls all around them.

McQuade waited. Maksim stopped suddenly. He had moved, McQuade realized. The other man now stood about ten feet further into the tunnel. McQuade turned towards the sound of his voice.

"The steel case contains a flag, Lieutenant – a very special, very precious flag."

"A flag?" McQuade was incredulous.

"Yes."

"Is it made of gold?" the American pilot asked quite seriously.

"No. But it is different and more precious than any other flag, nonetheless."

"How? What makes it so special that you and the two uniformed soldiers accompanying you would guard it with your lives?"

The silence came again and then Maksim lit his cigarette lighter. The sudden flare of the flame made McQuade wince and blink his eyes. Under the soft glow of the light the Ukrainian looked haggard, the planes of his face sallow and hacked through with deeply chiseled lines. He beckoned McQuade closer and the two men sat with their backs against the tunnel wall, their heads close together so the words could be whispered.

After a long time, Maksim began to talk, sounding like a man about to share a long story.

"Do you know the colors of the Ukrainian flag, Lieutenant?"

"No," McQuade confessed and felt unaccountably guilty for the admission. "To be honest, I didn't even really know where your country was until the war broke out."

The Ukrainian history professor grunted. "You Americans are all alike," he could not conceal the gentle bitterness in his voice. "You think your country is the center of the world." He sighed and shifted his weight, stretching his legs out in front of him. "The Ukraine flag is a horizontal panel of blue above a horizontal panel of yellow. The blue represents the sky, the streams and the mountains. The yellow symbolizes wheat. But it was not always so. Thousands of years before Ukraine existed, this region was known as Kievan Rus, and both Ukraine and Russia can trace their origins back to that state. Kievan Rus began back in the tenth century, on the banks of Dnipro. There were flags in those days, but no record of their design exists. All that we know is that a trident head was used as a symbol of the nation.

"The earliest known flag of Ukraine was the swallow-tailed flag of the Polish-Lithuanian Commonwealth, which was established in 1587, following the unification of the Kingdom of Poland with the Grand Duchy of Lithuania. But from 1772, the flag of the Habsburg monarchy was hoisted because the territory had come under Austrian rule. The flag was black and yellow horizontal stripes."

Maksim paused in his telling to reach into his coat pocket for a cigarette. He offered one to McQuade then lit them both. The two men smoked in silence for a few moments. Maksim blew a thin feather of smoke into the darkness.

"But in 1848, brave revolutionaries fighting a war for independence in the west of Ukraine defiantly adopted a new flag that consisted of a bi-colored blue and yellow horizontal striped flag. The revolutionary movement chose those colors based on the coat of arms that was being used by the city of Lviv at the time which included a golden lion on a blue shield. One of the revolutionaries was a heroic man named Yevhen Volodymirovich Levytsk. His name appears in no history books but he was an organizer of the revolutionaries… and the man who stitched the first revolutionary flag. For years that blue and yellow banner was a rallying symbol for all free men who fought for liberty. It was a call to patriots that could be seen for miles far and wide."

McQuade finished his cigarette and crushed the butt beneath his boot. "Until?"

"Until the Soviets invaded the territory in 1919," Maksim's tone became harsh, like a man recalling a bitter memory. "Ukraine became the Ukrainian Soviet Socialist Republic. All territorial flags were banned. A Soviet flag hung from our government buildings. It was not until we gained our independence in 1992 that the beloved blue and yellow colors were once again a symbol of Ukraine."

McQuade forced himself to his feet and stretched some of the stiffness from his weary body. "You still haven't told me what's in the steel case," he prodded.

"It's the original flag of the 1848 revolutionaries," Maksim said softly. "It is the original flag that Yevhen Volodymirovich Levytsk hand stitched."

McQuade felt a twinge of disappointment that the contents of the metal case was not some precious jewel or ancient golden trinket. "So how did you find it?"

"I didn't," Maksim said. "The flag was entrusted to me."

"You inherited it?"

"No," the Ukrainian professor shook his head. "It is a priceless historical treasure. It was presented to my university many years ago. When the Russians invaded, I was charged with its safe keeping and given two guards. I was told to spirit the flag across the border to the west where it would be safe."

"Well, you're going the wrong way," McQuade tried to make light of the tense, almost supernatural moment. He felt uneasy.

"No. I'm going another way," Maksim corrected. "I'm not fleeing with the flag. Instead, I am taking it south to the *Svyatynya heroyam Ukrayiny:* the 'Shrine to Heroes of Ukraine'."

"A shrine?"

"*The* Shrine to Heroes of Ukraine," Maksim corrected. "It is a plaza ten miles to the south of here, filled with statues and monuments. It was built after the Second World War to commemorate all the heroic Ukrainian soldiers who fought and died in war."

"Why take it there?"

"The plaza is a vast open space surrounded by several military museums and buildings of historical significance. The most important building is the 'Shrine to Heroes' that stands on the southern edge of the square. Atop the Shrine, Lieutenant, is a flagpole that has not borne a flag for seventy years."

McQuade frowned. "You want to hang *your* flag there?"

"Yes!" Maksim was suddenly alive with passion. His eyes flashed with the fervor of a zealot. "I want to hang the flag of the revolutionaries from that flagpole so that its message and rally cry will be seen and known across the land. I want to unite the Ukraine fighters at war with the Russians. I want to remind our heroic soldiers of their origins, their heritage – and rekindle the unquenchable thirst for freedom that will spark the determination to drive every Russian soldier from Ukraine."

McQuade said nothing for a long moment. In the darkness he was frowning.

"But it's just a flag…"

"No!" Maksim snapped. "It is a symbol, Lieutenant. Hanging from that flagpole it becomes a beacon of defiance and of liberty. It has the power to unite us and fill every proud Ukrainian's heart with steel."

"Why are *you* doing this?"

"I have told you already; for Ukraine, for freedom… and for my children." He reached into his pocket and produced a creased, stained polaroid. He flicked on his cigarette lighter and showed the photograph to McQuade. "They are my son and daughter. He is an engineer in Germany. My daughter, Katya, is a doctor. She lives in the south of the country."

"And what about the refugees with you? What happens to them when you try to raise your flag and the Russians attempt to stop you?"

The Ukrainian professor's tone hardened. "Each of the people in our small group has lost loved ones. Each of their hearts beats with the same love of Ukraine. They come to avenge their families and friends. They come because there is nowhere else to go and no other way for them to fight back. Surely you have family, Lieutenant. Surely you can understand?"

"No," McQuade shook his head and his voice turned hollow. "I haven't seen or spoken to my parents for years…"

Maksim's voice became pitying. "You are an empty man, Lieutenant. You have shunned God, ignored history, and forsaken your family. I feel sorry for you. Until you find something greater than yourself to care about and to sacrifice for, you will forever be selfish and insignificant."

They sat in feuding silence for several minutes, listening to Russian artillery overhead. The shells were landing somewhere to the north, the vibration of each explosion sending little tremors through the earth. Finally, Maksim forced himself to his feet and grunted. "I have much to do. I suggest you rest while you can, American. When night comes, we will continue our journey south."

The Ukrainian turned and walked back down the long tunnel. McQuade watched him go. A Russian artillery shell landed somewhere nearby. The shock of the explosion caused a trickle of earth to leak from the tunnel's ceiling and grey dust hung in the air. A second later another shell landed directly overhead, exploding through the roof of the tractor plant.

*

With a crack like a gunshot, the concrete ceiling of the tunnel fractured and dust poured like smoke from the fissure. McQuade scrambled to his feet. He began to run, infected by terror, fear slithering in his guts. Another crack, this one louder, sounded directly over his head. McQuade blundered on, the blood humming in his ears. A hundred yards ahead of him, through the swirling dust, he could see Maksim and the rest of the refugees scrambling in terror-stricken panic to reach the steps.

The tunnel wall to his left groaned and then seemed to bulge. In front of him a giant slab of concrete broke away from the ceiling and crashed to the ground. McQuade heard himself sobbing with desperation and fear. The tunnel turned thick with smothering dust. Loose rocks and chunks of concrete began to fall from the ceiling. One struck him a glancing blow on the shoulder. A bolt of white-hot pain shot down the length of his arm. He staggered against the tunnel wall and it seemed that the earth around him growled.

He realized with sudden sickening despair that he wouldn't make it, but he forced himself on, his feet turning to lead, the dust choking in his throat. He pressed his hand against the tunnel wall and ran on blindly in the dark and the swirling haze.

Another piece of concrete crashed to the ground. The ceiling overhead seemed to sag. He cried out in desperation and heard his own voice echo off the walls. With a deafening roar the tunnel in front of him collapsed. McQuade threw himself down and scrambled beneath a huge slab of shattered cement that had fallen to the ground and lay leaning against the wall. He tucked his knees to his chest and rolled onto his side. The dark was absolute, the world a deafening roar of destruction that seemed to go on forever. He clenched his jaw and stifled a scream of terror until, at last, the cacophony of the collapsing tunnel subsided and there were just the sounds of shifting rubble and the thump of his racing heart.

*

The oppressive darkness was like a lead weight that squeezed down on McQuade as he huddled in his tiny shelter. There was no room to move, other than to extend his legs, and the dust was something solid that he inhaled and choked on. He covered his mouth and nose with his hand; taking shallow breaths until his heart stopped pounding and the dust finally settled.

All that stood between him and being crushed to death was the long slab of concrete pitched against the wall. He groped with his fingers around the few inches of space. He felt like he had been buried alive – and that terrifying thought started a wave of panic.

Fear rose as a lump in his chest, strangling him.

Distract yourself! Keep your mind occupied.

He felt over the pockets of his survival vest, taking an inventory of the meagre possessions he carried with him. Then he thought about flying, and behind his closed eyes he visualized the cockpit of his Viper. Starting with the left side controls, he listed each one and explained their purpose like he was giving a lecture, talking aloud because the sound of the silence was soul-destroying.

When he had itemized every control and switch in the fighter's cockpit, his thoughts turned to Maksim and the refugees. He replayed the Ukrainian's explanation about the flag of the revolutionaries and remembered his stinging words.

"You are an empty man, Lieutenant. You have shunned God, ignored history, and forsaken your family. I feel sorry for you. Until you find something greater than yourself to care about and to sacrifice for, you will forever be selfish and insignificant."

He tried to conjure up an image of his parents, but they were nothing more than vague memories, indistinct and without definition. He wondered idly what Maksim's God looked like…

"If I get out of here, I'll be different," he vowed.

And then his train of thought was interrupted by a faint tap.

McQuade stiffened and held his breath.

Tap… tap… tap…

He fumbled on the ground for a rock but could feel nothing. With frantic fingers he wriggled his hand inside his flying suit and withdrew the Beretta. He turned the gun around and rapped three times against the concrete with the butt then listened intently in the heavy silence.

Tap… tap… tap…

"Thank God!" he wheezed. The tight steel band of tension constricting his chest eased and he drew a deep shuddering breath of relief. "Thank God!"

*

Maksim and the two uniformed soldiers stood before the wall of broken concrete and bricks that had sealed the tunnel and turned to each other.

"He's alive," Maksim said. The three spaced taps had come loud and sharp from somewhere within the rubble. "We have to dig him out."

He peeled off his grubby stained jacket and rolled up the sleeves of his shirt. The two soldiers stripped to the waist. One of the men had found an iron girder on the factory floor. They used it like a crow bar to lever the heavy slabs aside and then attacked the loose debris with their bare hands. Behind them, the refugees lit candles and waited in grim, anxious silence.

For two hours the three men toiled at the back-breaking work, removing each brick, stone, and chunk of concrete one piece at a time and carrying it away from the rock face. Maksim's body ached and his hands had been stripped raw and bloody. He was lathered in sweat and breathing hard. He reeled away from the rubble and leaned against the tunnel wall to hold himself upright. He estimated they had cleared away about ten feet of debris. One of the women came down the passageway with a pail of rainwater. Maksim drank greedily and then passed the water to the soldiers. More men came forward to take their turn working shoulder-to-shoulder at the rock face.

"We must be close," Maksim said, almost in despair. The words rasped across his throat. He picked up a nearby brick and went to the high mound of debris. He struck the brick against a concrete block three times.

The reply from within the collapsed tunnel was almost instantaneous, and very close.

Tap! Tap! Tap!

"He's here!" Maksim furrowed his brow and listened carefully to the sound like a bloodhound picking up the scent. "It's coming from over here!"

The two young soldiers came back to the wall of stone and waded into the rubble with renewed urgency. No longer wasting time to clear away each piece, they burrowed into the tumble of rock, tearing nails from their bloody fingertips in their frantic haste. Maksim urged them on, his voice imploring them to hurry.

From beneath a layer of loose earth and broken stone the edge of a long slab of concrete emerged, standing almost upright against the tunnel wall. The two soldiers dug down and removed a pile of crushed bricks. Then a hand suddenly thrust from the wreckage, grey with dust, scratched and bleeding. The hand clenched into a fist and McQuade's voice carried to them through a small dark opening, reedy and hoarse.

"I'm here!"

*

The two soldiers carried McQuade like a sack of wheat and laid him out on the tunnel floor, close to the stairs. His injuries were superficial. Maksim held a mug of water to his lips and he drank thirstily, then choked. One of the women dabbed at his cuts and scrapes with a damp rag.

"You were lucky, American," Maksim said gravely. "God was watching over you, I think."

McQuade said nothing.

Late in the afternoon the refugees began gathering up their meagre belongings, preparing themselves for the arduous night's journey that lay ahead. Maksim prowled around the tunnel entrance like a caged lion, impatient for night, but also growing tense with anxiety. He spoke with the two uniformed soldiers at length and then stiffened and nodded his head, as though a decision had been made. He gathered the refugees around him and smiled benign encouragement at them like a watchful shepherd over his flock of sheep.

"We will wait until darkness before we set out on the next leg of our journey," he announced. "In the meantime, I will go out into the city ruins to search for more food. While I am gone, Oleksandr will be in charge. All of you should be ready to move the moment I return."

He went up the stairs with the two soldiers following him. Some instinct made McQuade follow. He hauled himself to his feet and took a few tottering steps until his balance returned. He walked like an old man, wincing and using the handrail to haul himself up the staircase.

The tractor factory had taken three direct hits from Russian artillery. McQuade could see the exact spot where he had been buried alive; the factory floor had collapsed like a sinkhole. He steered a wide berth and saw that two more shells had struck the damaged western end of the vast building. Part of the structure and a row of workshop offices had been destroyed. Glass and rubble crunched underfoot as he followed Maksim and the guards to the far end of the factory.

Night was still an hour away, but the afternoon had turned overcast and gloomy, the sky steel-grey and heavy with rainclouds. Maksim picked a route through the bomb-ruined debris, then turned back to issue his final instructions.

"If I am not back in an hour, go on without me," he told the soldiers. "You know what must be done. Ukraine is depending on us."

He stepped out of the shadows of the factory and set out along a cratered alleyway. McQuade watched him walk to an intersection, then turn left. Far away in the distance the Russian artillery still rumbled, and from surrounding streets came the sporadic fire of automatic weapons. Thunder rolled across the sky and the clouds seemed to sink lower, reflecting the orange glow of fires that burned throughout the devastated city.

The three men began a silent vigil, waiting for Maksim's return. It began to rain; a soft gentle pearlescent haze turned into persistent showers that puddled in the shell craters and turned dust to mud. After thirty minutes a Russian Army troop truck drove through the intersection, its engine in low gear, belching diesel exhaust. It passed out of sight and then McQuade heard a sharp squeal of brakes. He glanced ominously at the two soldiers who crouched low in the shadows.

Suddenly six Russian soldiers appeared at the corner of the crossroad. They were grimy and disheveled; their boots and uniforms smeared with mud. One of the soldiers pointed towards the tractor factory and the rest of the patrol followed.

"Christ!" McQuade whispered. "They're coming this way."

The alley was a few hundred yards of cratered, weed-strewn tarmac, bordered on either side by chainmail fence.

The two Ukrainian soldiers exchanged worried glances.

"Do we fight them?" McQuade asked and drew his Beretta.

"No," the soldier named Oleksandr made a decision. "We get back down into the tunnels and hide. Quickly!"

The three men fell back into the shadows, weaving their way like ghosts across the debris-littered factory floor. They swarmed down the stairs and herded the refugees deeper into the darkness of the tunnel. McQuade and Oleksandr stayed at the foot of the stairs, then backed away into the blackness as the sound of the Russians grew closer overhead.

McQuade could hear the scuff of their boots as they searched the factory. Then he could hear voices, grumbling and discontent.

"K chertu eto! My zrya teryayem vremya!"

"He says this is a waste of fucking time," Oleksandr whispered in McQuade's ear, then there was a splashing sound as one of the Russians urinated. Another soldier kicked something metallic that skidded across the floor and crashed against a wall. There was another brief snarl of chatter and then the sounds of footsteps receded. McQuade, crouching at the mouth of the tunnel in the darkness, came slowly to his feet and took a few tentative paces towards the stairs. He listened carefully, frowning, and then said cautiously, "I think they've gone."

With Oleksandr at his side, McQuade went quietly up the steps. The factory was dark and gloomy, the approaching night falling like a blanket. A harsh shouted voice of command from somewhere in the night chilled their blood.

They dashed across the factory floor. McQuade was overcome with a sudden sickening slide of terrible foreboding.

They reached the ruined western end of the factory and peered warily out into the approaching night. The six Russian soldiers who had searched the factory were now standing at the intersection in a tight knot, their weapons raised – at Maksim.

"Christ!" McQuade breathed and felt the blood drain away from his face.

Maksim stood with his hands high in the air. At his feet was a small cloth wrapped bundle. Two of the Russian soldiers stood either side of the Ukrainian professor, guarding him. One of the Russians stepped forward and eyed Maksim suspiciously. His voice was loud and authoritative, and carried clearly to where McQuade and Oleksandr watched on with rising dread.

The Russian drew a handgun from his holster and extended his arm until the muzzle of the weapon was pressed hard against Maksim's forehead.

"Who are you? Where are you going?" Oleksandr translated the guttural Russian questions for McQuade's benefit.

"My name is Maksim Guslistaya," the Ukrainian replied, his voice calm and pitched high with a protest of innocence. "I am going to my home."

"Where do you live? Where are your papers?"

Maksim rattled off an address. The Russian looked suspicious.

"Do you know there is a strict curfew across the city? Anyone not indoors by nightfall will be shot," the Russian said.

"Yes," Maksim bobbed his head obsequiously. "That was why I was hurrying to my home when you stopped me, officer."

The Russian holding the gun to Maksim's head looked down at the ground and nudged the cloth-wrapped bundle with the toe of his boot. "And what are you concealing from us, pig? Do you carry explosives? Are you a partisan bastard?"

Maksim shook his head. He looked terrified. His face was pale, his eyes huge.

"I am a teacher," he professed his innocence. His hands over his head began to shake. "The parcel contains just some bread and tinned food I found in the ruins. I was taking it home to my elderly mother. She is unwell, and I…"

The Russian changed his grip on the pistol and hit Maksim hard across the face. The butt of the weapon slashed the man's cheek open and bright red blood spilled down his face, soaking the collar of his rumpled suit. Maksim grunted in pain and took a staggered step backwards. He clamped his hand to his cheek and the blood ran through his fingers.

The Russian barked a short brusque command. One of the other soldiers in the patrol stepped forward and prodded the cloth-wrapped bundle suspiciously with the barrel of his rifle. A loaf of bread and two cans spilled onto the ground.

"You would steal this food from Russian soldiers?" the Russian officer with the handgun seemed suddenly enraged. He glared an accusation at Maksim and waved the pistol in front of his face menacingly so the barrel weaved like a cobra dancing to the tune of a charmer.

"No," Maksim made his voice weak and blubbering. He sagged at the knees and one of the Russian guards hooked a hand beneath his armpit to force him upright. "I stole nothing. I found the food in the ruins."

"Jesus Christ!" McQuade whispered hoarsely. "They're going to fucking kill him! Do something!" He raised the Beretta and took aim at the Russian officer but Oleksandr swatted the handgun roughly aside.

"No! We do nothing," he hissed grimly. "If we open fire, we're all dead."

The Russian officer kicked the cans of food into the mud and crushed the loaf of bread under his boot, grinding it into the dirt. "There, Ukraine pig. You're all filthy animals. It should not bother you to eat from the ground."

A couple of the soldiers in the patrol laughed callously. The Russian officer stepped back from Maksim and holstered his weapon. For a moment the tense scene seemed to balance on a knife-edge. McQuade held his breath. Then, with a sudden explosion of rage and a snarl of bitter hatred, the Russian officer kicked Maksim hard in the stomach.

The Ukrainian man folded forward, the air driven from his lungs. He collapsed on the ground, gasping painfully for breath. The Russian officer kicked him several more times. Maksim tucked himself into a ball and covered his head with his hands.

Finally, the Russian stepped back, breathing deeply, and stared down at the sobbing man in the dirt.

"Let this be a warning to you. You are vermin. You are filth – your life means nothing to me. Now scurry back to your rat hole before I put a bullet between your eyes."

The patrol moved off. The Russians swaggered back to their waiting troop truck. Maksim dragged himself to his feet, one arm wrapped across his chest. His suit coat was filthy with mud and blood. He took a few staggering steps and then leaned against the chainmail fencing to catch his breath.

McQuade leaped impulsively to his feet to go to Maksim's aid, but again Oleksandr pushed him roughly back down into the shadows.

"Do not move," the Ukrainian soldier warned. "The Russian patrol could still be watching. If it's a trap, you will get us all shot. Wait. Maksim must come to us. Until then we do nothing but watch."

McQuade glared at the soldier. "You ruthless bastard," he growled. "The man is in pain. He's just been beaten."

"Yes. But he is still alive, and so are we. Survival is everything."

It took an agonizing ten minutes for Maksim to stagger the few hundred yards into the shadows of the tractor factory. By then night had fallen across the city and the rain had begun to pour in torrents. The Ukrainian was soaked and battered and bleeding, his breath coming in short gasping wheezes that seemed to rattle from his lungs. He slumped down in the burned ruins and Oleksandr went to him.

"Are your ribs broken?" the soldier carefully peeled off the older man's sodden coat.

"No," Maksim shook his head. He drew a deep shuddering breath and winced. Oleksandr motioned to McQuade. "Drape his arm around your shoulder. We must get him down into the tunnels."

"No," Maksim shrugged the helping hands away. "Send for the rest of the group. We must leave here immediately. The night and the rain will conceal our movements."

"But Maksim..!" Oleksandr protested.

"Do as I say," the injured man growled.

The refugees came up the stairs in single file, their belongings in their arms, their ancient weapons slung over their shoulders. Maksim propped himself upright against a pylon and spoke quickly.

"We must flee from here immediately and continue southwards. I urge you to leave anything unnecessary behind. Carry only what is essential. The journey tonight will be difficult, and there will be little opportunity to rest. Oleksandr," Maksim grunted, "lead the way."

Chapter 6:

With the two Ukraine soldiers in the vanguard, the rest of the bedraggled refugees followed in single file. They made a miserable procession, moving cautiously in the darkness, their path lit by just the stars and the glow of raging fires. Their route took them south through a precinct of low-income apartment complexes, and across an abandoned industrial estate of small warehouse buildings.

Oleksandr carried the steel case tucked inside his uniform jacket, the chain dangling from the handcuff attached to his wrist. Maksim walked amidst the column of refugees, his steps slow and shuffling, his weight on a length of steel pipe he used like a walking stick.

McQuade drifted back through the column until he found himself walking beside the woman who had stared at him so brazenly and defiantly in the cellar; the woman he had crossed the road alongside and covered with his body when the Russian eight-wheeled APC had almost discovered them.

He watched the young woman covertly from the corner of his eye as they walked. She wore stained and faded denim jeans and a scruffy parker over a sweater. Her dirty blonde hair was scraped back from her face and gathered in a pony tail. Over her shoulder was slung a battered old bolt-action rifle with a telescopic sight.

They reached a laneway between two apartment buildings. To the west of where they stood an entire city block seemed to be on fire. The flames lit up the night forcing the refugees to pick a path through the shadows. A thick blanket of black choking smoke rolled over them.

"You have no children with you," McQuade said.

"No," the woman moved like a cat, lithe and silent.

"And no husband?"

The woman stopped and looked levelly at McQuade. "No. He was killed in the fighting against the Russians."

"I'm sorry," McQuade muttered. "Was he a soldier?"

"No, he was a doctor. Russian artillery shelled the city block where he was working. Many people were killed."

They cleared the laneway and began to wind a ragged path across a carpark of burned out and abandoned vehicles. Some were peppered with bullet holes. Others had been set on fire, the windows smashed and the seats slashed by scavengers.

"Why are you here?" McQuade persisted gently. "Why did you join Maksim's refugees? Is it to avenge the death of your husband?"

"I joined to avenge the deaths of the thousands of Ukraine men who have died in the war," she said, "and the thousands of women who have been murdered or raped… or worse…" her voice filled with zealous passion.

"What is your name?"

"Lyudmila," the woman said.

The refugee column reached the curb of a side street and the two soldiers dropped warily to their knees and raised their weapons. Lyudmila reacted instinctively, slipping the rifle off her shoulder and raising it. Her focus was absolute, her eyes dark and fixed. She scanned the far side of the street, searching the shadows for danger.

After thirty seconds of tense silence, Oleksandr rose slowly to his feet and waved the column forward. They went across the street in single file, always sticking to the shadows, creeping in the darkness to the shelter of a row of houses.

McQuade and Lyudmila crossed the street together. On the far side of the road she dropped to her knee and pulled the rifle butt into her shoulder, aiming along the barrel to cover the route they had taken. She stayed in position, wary and alert, until the two soldiers had traversed the road and the column could move on.

"Were you in the Ukraine military?" McQuade asked when they were walking again, heading towards an intersection where two trucks had collided and overturned. There was shattered glass across the blacktop and the strong smell of diesel. One of the vehicles had caught fire. The charred remains of two figures hung upside down in one of the vehicle's crumpled cabins. Flies swarmed around the corpses. "You move like a soldier."

"No," Lyudmila answered McQuade's question. "But my grandfather was. This is his rifle," she held it out for McQuade to see. In the darkness he saw very little. It looked like any other bolt-action rifle.

"He used it in the Second World War to kill Nazis, and he fought at the battle for Sevastopol. If you run your fingers over the stock, you will feel the notches," her voice said with fierce pride. "One for every enemy bastard he killed."

"And now you want to kill Russians with it?"

"Of course," her eyes hardened and she bridled. "You think I cannot shoot because I am a woman?"

"No," McQuade retreated.

"I can shoot, American," Lyudmila's voice hardened to steel. "And I have already killed four Russian soldiers. I will kill many more before the war is ended because until every enemy soldier is driven back across the border there can be no peace for us."

Unbidden, Lyudmila began to talk about Ukraine and her hopes for the nation, and there was a fanatical light in her dark eyes. She spoke with a compelling power and deep passion, articulating her vision for the future in a voice that was pitched low and husky. McQuade watched the shape of her mouth as she spoke, and the way she used her hands to emphasize each point. She reached into the pocket of her parka and took a cigarette from a crumpled packet. Still talking, she lit the cigarette and drew deeply, then exhaled with a sound like a sigh of frustration.

"We have for too long been denied our independence. Ukraine has spent too much time beneath the heel of its oppressors. Only a fierce independence movement, run by the people and governed by the people, can bring long term prosperity."

McQuade was unsettled by the force of the woman's fierce patriotic passion. The fervor in her eyes for Ukraine's cause seemed fanatical. For a long moment he looked at her, searching for signs of vanity or uncertainty, but only saw determination and resolve.

He was about to apologize to her when, from the head of the column, Oleksandr turned and hissed everyone to urgent silence. They were cowered in the shadows of a small block of units, surrounded by several tall trees. At the far end of the road, perhaps three hundred yards away, three Russian BMP-2 infantry fighting vehicles suddenly appeared, belching black plumes of diesel exhaust, their engines snarling. A white flare arced into the night sky, shining bright as the sun and bathing the entire length of the street in light.

"Down! Down on the ground!" Oleksandr hissed.

The three Russian armored troop carriers swerved onto the footpath and braked to a sudden halt. The rear doors of the vehicles swung open and a Platoon of Russian infantry emerged, moving with practiced alacrity. They formed a perimeter around the three APCs and McQuade saw an officer urging them on, waving his hand and barking sharp orders.

"Retreat into the building!" Maksim whispered. "Quickly!"

*

"Are they searching for us?" McQuade wanted to know as the refugees swarmed in through the narrow doorways of the building. There were two units on the ground floor and two more above, connected by an external flight of stairs. Oleksandr, McQuade and Lyudmila crept up the steps, seeking an elevated platform from which to defend themselves.

"I don't know!" Oleksandr hissed. Downstairs they could hear Maksim herd the rest of the refugees into a room on the far side of the building, his voice calm and reassuring despite the perilous danger of the situation. The rest of the men in the group were on the ground floor, standing guard at the windows with the other Ukraine soldier organizing them.

McQuade crept cautiously to a window and peered down along the street.

The Russians had not moved. They were facing across the road, the turrets of the APCs turned in that direction also.

None of the soldiers had patrolled closer to their hiding place. Then a smattering of gunfire broke out, coming from further down the street. It was undisciplined shooting; a chatter of automatic weapon rounds punctuated by single round '*crack!*'s that echoed across the dark night.

"They're partisans," Oleksandr cocked his ear for a moment.

"How can you tell?"

"The weapons," the Ukraine soldier said, and held up his own assault rifle. "The AK-74 is standard issue for troops in the Ukraine Army. Some of them are firing with rifles…"

The Russians punched back with a fury of overwhelming firepower. The turret-mounted 30mm autocannons on the APCs roared, and long tongues of flame from their barrels lit up the night in flickering fire. The Russian infantry sprang into action, moving with the synchronized precision that comes from long hours of rehearsed combat drills. Half a dozen of the soldiers dispersed to the edges of the perimeter to give covering fire while the rest went forward across the street, shooting from their hips as they advanced. The noise of the firefight reached a thundering crescendo.

McQuade saw one Russian soldier go down, shot in the face. The impact of the bullet snapped the man's head back and sent his helmet spinning in the air. He fell to the ground, the contents of his skull just a pink puff of mist.

Another flare arced across the night sky, casting the battlefield in momentary stark light. The Russians stormed across the street and spread out along the footpath facing a row of bomb-ravaged suburban houses. The partisans were holding the first line of buildings, firing without the discipline of the Russians, but still throwing down enough fury to keep the enemy at arm's length. McQuade saw a Russian soldier make a throwing motion and a few seconds later the sound of an exploding grenade shook the night. One of the houses the partisans were defending burst into flames and then a feather of fire streaked across the night with a roar of noise and a wicked slithering hiss. A cloud of white smoke drifted over the street. The feather of flame flashed from within the darkened window of a house and lanced towards the closest Russian armored troop carrier. The RPG rocket blew the BMP-2 into a thousand steel fragments, enveloping it in a fierce fireball of flames.

"Jesus!" McQuade flinched and ducked down behind the window, aghast. "The partisans just blew one of the Russian APCs to pieces. We're caught right in the middle of a major fucking fight!"

Lyudmila poked her head above the window and studied the battlefield. Three Russian soldiers were down, writhing and rolling in agony on the tarmac. The destroyed BMP-2 was a crumpled wreck of twisted metal. Black boiling smoke billowed into the night sky. The scene was lit by flashes of light against a backdrop of staccato gunfire. She slid the rifle off her shoulder and propped the barrel on the windowsill to steady her aim.

"What are you doing?" McQuade was mortified. "You'll give away our position."

"We have to help the partisans," Lyudmila said coldly. "They are our brothers and sisters."

Taking careful aim on one of the Russians kneeling on the footpath, she waited patiently until a flurry of automatic fire ripped the night apart. She squeezed the trigger and the weapon kicked viciously against her shoulder. Working the bolt with cool composure, she chambered another round and searched the battlefield for the Russian officer.

Lyudmila saw him at last. He was crouched behind a brick fence, waving his men forward and barking orders. One of the partisans in the row of houses must have fired in his direction, for he ducked suddenly and covered his head with his hands. Lyudmila waited. McQuade watched her face with macabre fascination. Her eyes were blank, her expression cold and impassive. He saw a tiny frown crease between her eyes and then the rifle bucked and kicked, and the *'crack!'* of the weapon's retort filled the tiny room with its roar.

"Dead," she announced with malicious satisfaction. "Another bastard sent to hell."

She chambered another round and took aim at one of the injured Russian soldiers sprawled on the blacktop, still twisting in pain. The man lay on his back, clutching at a bloody thigh wound. Maksim's voice from the far side of the room made her pause.

"Downstairs, all of you. Right now! We're leaving."

"But the partisans – " Lyudmila began to protest.

"Their fight is not our fight," Maksim scolded her. "They fight for today, and we are fighting for our nation's future. The only thing that matters is raising the flag above *Svyatynya heroyam Ukrayiny.*"

Lyudmila shouldered her weapon and bit down on her protest. She nodded her head in guilty acquiescence. They crept down the stairs together and spilled out onto the sidewalk, using the façade of the apartment units as a shield between them at the Russians at the far end of the street. Maksim herded everyone into a pool of dark shadow. "We must detour around the fighting and then turn south again. We must go now, while the Russians are occupied, and before they can call up reinforcements. Stick to the shadows and move quickly. We will not stop to rest for many hours."

*

The detour around the fighting forced the refugees several blocks west. It was an unfamiliar part of the city to Maksim and he became cautious, sending the two uniformed soldiers forward to scout the way ahead whenever they reached a street corner.

The children in the straggling group became tired and restless. Tension and strain weighed down on everyone. Tempers began to fray as the night wore on and the looming danger of daylight grew inevitably closer.

They reached an intersection and Maksim, once again, called a cautious halt. The group pressed against a fence and cowered in the shadows while he went forward to the corner and gnawed indecisively on his lower lip. To continue in their current direction would take them through a narrow street, lined on both sides by shops that had been devastated by Russian artillery fire. To turn south would force them too close to the enemy soldiers fighting the partisans. By now the Russians would have called up reinforcements, and would have blocked off the entire precinct with APCs and additional troops.

"I know this area," Lyudmila volunteered. She came forward out of the shadows and knelt close to Maksim. "It is my grandmother's old street. She lived in an apartment above the grocery store before the war started. I can go forward."

Maksim peered down the length of the dark shadow-struck road. There were no two-story buildings still standing. Every structure along the little shopping strip had been reduced to rubble. His frown deepened, and he turned and looked south again with forlorn longing. The sounds of fighting still carried on the night and the sky was criss-crossed with flares and drifting smoke.

"Very well," he muttered. "But go carefully."

Maksim was unhappy. The lure of the quicker route south still goaded him and he cursed under his breath, bitter because the handful of partisans had kicked up a hornet's nest of Russian troops and thus made his journey more dangerous. The refugees in his care were exhausted, and his meticulous plan had come unraveled. Until he could swing south once more and continue along his pre-planned route, he felt an unsettled sense of ominous foreboding.

The street was eerily silent. The night's stars were hidden behind drifting curtains of smoke that darkened the sky and veiled everything beneath a grey haze. He sniffed the air. There would be rain tomorrow, he judged, and that made the need to find a place to hide-up throughout the day even more urgent. Many of the refugees – especially the children – were sickly with exhaustion.

Maksim went back over the original route he had planned to reach the 'Shrine to Heroes of Ukraine' in his head, and then visualized how far west their detour had forced them, trying to calculate a course that would re-connect the refugees with their destination. If there was an intersection that led south at the end of the shopping district, he decided, he would take it. Oleksandr crouched in the shadows beside him, thinking similar thoughts.

"The Russians will quickly crush the partisans."

"Yes."

"In an hour the fighting will be over and the Russians will pull their APCs back to their base for the night, leaving just small patrols on the street until morning."

"Yes."

"Then we can turn south again."

"Yes."

For a moment there was silence and then Oleksandr nodded towards Lyudmila. She was in the process of peeling off her heavy parka and stuffing a handful of ammunition into the pocket of her jeans.

"Are you sure you don't want me to scout ahead?" Oleksandr prompted.

"No. Lyudmila knows the street," Maksim said.

Oleksandr grunted. Maksim peered into the night one final time, quartering the narrow street with his eyes. He saw no movement, no sound that presaged menace.

Lyudmila went forward cautiously along the footpath, clinging to the shadows of a fence. The road ahead rose up a gentle incline, the shopfronts on either side sandwiched together. The sidewalks were choked with debris; timber fixtures, twisted metal, shattered glass and broken bricks lay strewn onto the road. A white sedan, parked on the opposite side of the road had all its windows smashed in, the panel work scorched by flames.

Lyudmila was forced away from the fence and out of the shadows by the debris. She stepped carefully, edging towards the center of the road to find a clear path forward. Gravel and shards of glass crunched loudly beneath her boots.

She held the rifle pulled tight to her shoulder, swinging the weapon to match the twists and turns of her body, sighting along the barrel in the direction she faced. Before the war, several of the buildings had been two-story structures comprising a small unit on the top floor and a shopfront on the ground floor. Russian artillery had devastated the street. Awnings hung sagging from bent frames, shop signs were peppered with shrapnel. Lyudmila stepped delicately through the debris outside a small dress shop. The interior had been gutted by fire, the ceiling collapsed so that the contents of the upstairs apartment had crashed through to the ground floor. She thought, with a gruesome jarring shock, that there were bodies scattered in the shadows but they were dress mannequins, burnt and blackened by fire.

Some of the buildings still smoldered. Smoke drifted across the street and caught in her throat. She accidentally kicked something metallic and it skittered across the abandoned street. A steel vice of alarm clamped tight around Lyudmila's heart. She froze and dropped into a crouch to make herself smaller. Her eyes hunted the landscape, looking for movement. She stayed like that for a full minute, fighting to control the pounding beat of her heart. Her mouth turned dry. Finally, she rose to her feet and moved on, with the fear still crawling beneath her skin.

The shattering impact of the artillery had leveled buildings and gutted others. A grocery store had both its plate glass windows blown in, the awning over the front door ripped to tatters. The contents of the shop were strewn across the footpath and road, blown out by the force of the direct hit. Upturned pieces of broken furniture and a cash register lay in the middle of the blacktop. Rotting fruit, thick with flies and crawling with rats lay spoiling. A delivery van had been overturned by the force of an explosion. It lay on its side, the panel work crumpled, the windshield shattered. The rear door of the van had been blown open, revealing a jumble of dead flowers inside.

Lyudmila edged around the carnage and stepped through a thick veil of billowing smoke. She heard something move to her right and she went suddenly very still. She turned her head slowly towards the sound, swinging the rifle as she moved until she was staring into the black shadowed void of a shoe shop. She squinted. The drifting smoke made her eyes water. She bent at the knees and shrunk her shoulders. The interior of the shop was black as ink. Lyudmila licked dry lips and began to edge backwards. Some primal instinct warned her there was danger in the darkness and she took a pace away, then another until she was almost on the opposite side of the road.

Then she screamed.

*

"What's happening?" McQuade's voice was urgent with alarm. The scream was abruptly cut off and the silent dark night slammed down again.

"I… I don't know…" Maksim fretted.

McQuade's instincts were roaring at him. He turned and nudged Oleksandr. "What did you see?"

"Lyudmila is in trouble."

"What's happened?"

Oleksandr pointed down the street. McQuade peered hard but the smoke obscured the night's meager light so that everything was a dull and indistinct silhouette. "She was walking towards a shopfront and then backed away…"

"And then what?" McQuade hissed, suppressing the urge to shout.

"And then someone came from the opposite side of the road and seized her."

"She's been captured?" McQuade felt a sick slide of dismay in his guts.

"Yes," the Ukrainian soldier's voice was grim. "I think they were Russian Special Operations Forces. They have two companies in the city, organized into 'death squads' to terrorize the partisans."

"What makes you so sure…?" Maksim began.

"The silhouette of the figure and the way he moved," Oleksandr shrugged when he heard his own explanation, realizing how flimsy his evidence was.

"Christ!" McQuade seethed and fumed his frustration. "Damn it to hell."

The sound of the young woman's piercing shrill scream had been heard by all the refugees. Some of the women in the group began to weep softly. The children, sensing this new despair, began to cry. Maksim turned and hissed at the shadows.

"Shut up!" He got irritably to his feet, and paced in the darkness, his head bowed, his shoulders hunched.

"Did you see where they took Lyudmila?" McQuade questioned Oleksandr.

"Into one of the buildings on the north side of the road," the soldier said.

"How many of them?"

"I only saw one silhouette."

McQuade bounced to his feet and turned on Maksim. "We have to go down there and rescue her," he said.

Maksim did not answer. He seemed torn by indecision. Finally, he folded his arms and shook his head grimly. "No," he said. "We must go on. The only thing that matters is reaching the 'Shrine to Heroes of Ukraine' and raising the flag of the revolutionaries."

"What? You would abandon Lyudmila to a Russian death squad? You know what they will do to her, Maksim!"

The Ukrainian professor flinched as if he had been stung by a slap across the face. For a moment he wavered and his eyes watered with tortured emotions. Then his expression became set and detached. "I have made up my mind. Lyudmila knew the chances and she was prepared to make any sacrifice necessary to free Ukraine. I will not risk the lives of many to save one. We must reach the Shrine."

McQuade lashed out.

"You fucking hypocritical, cowardly bastard!" he raged, his temper boiling over. "Since the moment you found me, you have lectured me about being selfish and about being a hollow empty man because I didn't know history. You criticized me because I did not believe in your God, and because I thought only about myself. Now I'm willing to risk my life to save one of *your* people, and you want to abandon her?" He thrust an accusing finger at Maksim and held it in his face like a threatening weapon. "You ought to be ashamed of yourself. Lyudmila, and people with her passion, are the best chance Ukraine has. She wants a future for this country. She wants peace and freedom. How can you walk away from someone who might one day change the fate of your nation?"

Maksim stood and felt each cutting word from McQuade erode and diminish him until he felt torn with embarrassed shame. He hung his head and the silence that followed was telling. McQuade waited for a rebuke that never came. The Ukrainian blinked, as though waking from a nightmare and then nodded slowly.

"Yes, American. You are right and I was wrong," he conceded shamefaced. "We must try to rescue her."

Oleksandr overheard and turned a mortified face on them. "You want to attempt to rescue her? We don't even know how many Russians are down there!"

"We will have to take that chance," Maksim conceded.

The Ukraine soldier wheeled on McQuade as if blaming him for the decision. "Will you be coming with us, American?" the sneered words were a direct challenge.

McQuade nodded his head grimly. "Yes," he said. "I will be leading the attack."

Chapter 7:

In the aftermath of his outburst of bravado, McQuade had quiet time to marvel at the aberration of attitude which had compelled him to propose the rescue. Maksim was right, he decided. The wise decision was to move on; to leave Lyudmila to the evil intent of the Russians. The soldiers most likely had already killed her, and a sensible man would turn south and make for the Shrine. Instead, impulsively, he had volunteered everyone's lives to save a woman he barely knew. He shook his head in admonishment and glanced sideways at where the two Ukraine soldiers, Maksim and three other men from the group were readying themselves. Oleksandr sensed he was being watched and glared levelly back. His lip curled into a snarl of contempt.

The men blackened their faces and hands with mud, then set off into the dark night in single file, weapons at the ready, the soldiers in the vanguard.

They reached the beginning of the bombed shopfronts and cut right, crossing the road and looking for a route behind the building-lined street.

Most of the businesses had been built backed on to narrow little lanes jostled by low, makeshift outbuildings that turned the route into a maze of alleyways and dark corners.

The approach in the darkness was painstaking. They stumbled on rubble, and black bags of rotting rubbish. They bumped into sharp corners and scuffed shins against low drainage ditches. Overhead the stars were beginning to fade before the approaching dawn and dark skeins of smoke hung in the still air. To the east, the sky was black with storm clouds, building ominously across the horizon.

The bomb-ravaged buildings took on gruesome, monstrous shapes of deep shadow and broken silhouettes. McQuade strained his senses for a sign that danger was nearby, or the telltale of a sentry. He sniffed the air for the scent of tobacco smoke, or the smell of cooking, but the night seemed utterly empty.

The sound of his breathing became hoarse and loud in his ears. He went following Maksim's footsteps, barely able to discern the man's outline in the inky blackness.

At every slight sound, the men were forced to stop and pause, tensed for the sudden wicked roar of an assault rifle or the challenge of a sentry. The moments dragged on until every step frayed their nerves and the night became an endless horror to be endured.

A sudden flare of light turned McQuade's churning guts to hot liquid.

"Down!" Oleksandr hissed.

They dropped to the ground or ducked into deep corners of shadow. McQuade crouched against the corner of a woodshed, his heart pounding in his chest and his hands wet with sweat. He searched the darkness and saw the light again, flickering, about twenty-five yards ahead.

The light was coming from a bomb-ruined building across the open space of an access alley. McQuade peered hard until, gradually, the scene before him materialized and made sense. The glow came from a burning candle, and the flickers he had seen were caused by figures moving across the light. The rear section of the building's brick wall had collapsed, but the rest of the wall facing McQuade appeared intact. He was staring through a smashed window into the room beyond.

He crawled forward on his hands and knees and pressed his mouth close to Maksim's ear.

"Lyudmila must be in there."

As if to confirm his suspicions a burst of raucous laughter split the night and someone gave a lustful growl. Then a voice spoke, carrying clearly in the stillness.

"Khvatit zhdat'. Ona nichego ne znayet. Yebat' suku."

"What did he say?" McQuade whispered.

"Lyudmila is in there and she is still alive," Maksim abbreviated, choosing not translate the crude message exactly. "They're going to rape her."

Before anyone in the group could restrain him, McQuade impulsively rose to his haunches and crept forward, bent double, clinging to the shadows. He crossed the alleyway with his teeth gritted, anticipating the loud retort of a gunshot and then the excruciating pain as the life bled out of him. He could hear every rustle of his flight suit, every gasp of his breath. He reached out for the wall. The alleyway stank of rotting garbage and corruption. He flattened himself against the cold bricks of the building. With his ear pressed to the wall he could hear movement inside; the shuffle of booted feet, the scrape of a piece of furniture and harsh breathing. He edged towards the window. He could feel his whole body strung tight with tension. He could hear the pounding of his blood in his ears, loud as a drum. He turned to face the brick wall and edged sideways until he stood close to the shattered window. There was broken glass on the ground. McQuade grimaced and clenched his jaw as he searched for a safe place to plant his feet. From the other side of the brick wall he heard a man laugh lecherously followed by the sound of fabric tearing. A woman made a muffled groan of protest and McQuade felt his blood boil as his imagination filled with a ghastly nightmare of graphic images.

He planted his foot and poked his head into the open window for just a split-second, then ducked down into the shadows. A moment had been enough. The images were seared into his mind, burned like a brand.

He crept back across the laneway, forcing himself to move with cautious restraint, but when he reached Maksim and the soldiers, the rage and loathing was upon him, blazing in his eyes.

He crouched down in the shadows close to Maksim and the two soldiers. His expression was terrible. "There are three Russian soldiers," he said. "They have Lyudmila tied on a tabletop. They're ripping the clothes off her. There is one man standing at the head of the table with his hand clamped over her mouth. There is another man standing guard at the front of the room, facing out onto the street. The third man…" he didn't need to say more.

"Where are their weapons?" Maksim asked.

McQuade closed his eyes and re-imagined the scene. "The soldier at the front of the room has an assault rifle," he said. "The other two men were unarmed."

Oleksandr grunted. He was fidgeting with nervous anticipation.

"Very well," Maksim nodded bleakly. He ordered the three other men in the group to remain in the alleyway to defend their retreat from any other Russians that might be within earshot and then got slowly to his feet. "We go now. American, you will cover the back of the building. I will go to the window. You two," he nodded at Oleksandr and his partner, "will assault the front of the building and take out the armed guard. Nobody moves until you hear my first shot."

They went like thieves, sweating with tension. Maksim crossed the alleyway and crouched beneath the shattered window, counting in his head to one hundred. To his right McQuade ran on. The rear of the building accessed the laneway via a wrought iron gate. It was open. McQuade sidled through and found himself standing in a small courtyard, not more than ten feet square. The ground was cracked concrete overgrown with weeds, leading up to two steps and a rear door into the building. The door hung off its hinges, splintered by shrapnel fragments. Something dark and disgusting scurried under his feet and disappeared down an open drain that reeked of raw sewerage. McQuade took the steps as if he were picking a path through a minefield, setting each toe down delicately, then slowly bringing his weight to bear. He reached the top step and pressed his ear against the shattered timber door. From somewhere beyond he could hear the muffled sound of voices.

He waited in the shadows, every nerve strung tight with tension. He felt sweat trickle down his back and the Beretta felt heavy in his hand. He tensed his body taut as a coiled spring and swallowed the lump of fear lodged in his throat.

Then suddenly he heard the abusively loud retort of a rifle shot and McQuade shouted to vent his fear as he put the weight of his shoulder against the door and heaved. The door collapsed inwards and a hail of debris fell down on him. He was in a dark narrow hallway, the walls lopsided and cracked from artillery damage. He stumbled over something hard, scraping skin off his shin, and then saw a flicker of light off to his left. He crashed forward and burst into the room where Lyudmila lay, half-naked on the table.

There was a Russian soldier standing with his back to him and another at the far end of the table between Lyudmila's splayed legs with his pants down around his thighs. McQuade snarled and raised the Beretta. The soldier at the far end of the table stood swaying on his feet, an expression of astonishment on his face. He was bleeding from a shoulder wound.

Everything seemed to still, and McQuade's senses detached from the horror of the moment. He noticed obscure details as if the fight were happening in slow motion. He saw the wounded man open his mouth to shout a warning, and the stubbled unshaven jaw of his sweating face as his head turned towards the shattered window. He saw an automatic rifle leaning against the edge of the table and the wounded soldier's hand instinctively reaching for it. He saw Lyudmila's long shapely legs, the flesh tanned and bleeding from a dozen shallow nicks where the Russians had cut away her jeans.

He threw the Beretta up and fired at the wounded Russian. He felt the handgun kick within his grip, the recoil throwing his hands high. The bullet struck the Russian in the open mouth and tore out through the back of the man's skull in a cloud of bright blood. His head snapped back, suddenly rubbery on the shoulders, and then he fell to the ground, already dead.

The Russian with his back to McQuade flung himself sideways with the reflexes of a jungle cat, diving for another assault rifle propped against the wall. McQuade snapped off a shot, missing the man completely. The Russian was screaming, bellowing fearfully at the top of his lungs. He landed hard on his shoulder and in a single fluid movement snatched up the assault rifle, pulled it close to his hip and swung the weapon onto McQuade. One of the candles in the room tipped over and a small fire started climbing up the wall. Flickering flames lit the darkness, turning the chaotic scene into something from a nightmare. McQuade threw himself down onto the ground and knew it was too little, too late. The Russian soldier saw McQuade hurl himself towards a dark shadowed corner and tracked him like a skeet shooter following the flight of the clay target.

McQuade hit the floor hard and the wind *whooshed* painfully from his lungs. He fired again across the room as his shoulder crashed into the floorboards, the sound deafeningly loud in the small confined space.

The Russian never fired. McQuade waited, tensed for the crushing agony of white-hot pain – but it never came. Instead, he saw Maksim, leaning in through the window, the rifle in his hands and the Russian dead on the ground, the side of his head shot away.

For a moment there was just heavy unholy silence – and then Oleksandr appeared from the shadows at the front of the building. He had a bloody knife in his hand. There was more blood splashed on the jacket of his uniform and up his wrist, dripping from the steel bracelet of the handcuff he wore. His expression was grim.

McQuade scrambled quickly to his feet. Lyudmila groaned groggily. Her face was bruised, the skin smeared from her lips, and her left eye was swollen. She turned her head slowly, like someone waking from a nightmare. Oleksandr crossed the room in three long strides.

Lyudmila had been bound wrist and ankle to the legs of the table with plastic cable ties. Oleksandr cut her free and then Maksim burst into the room, seeming to fill the confined space with his bulk. He peeled off his jacket and draped it over Lyudmila's shoulders. The woman seemed small and frail against him.

"We take everything useful and then we go – quickly," Maksim said.

McQuade snatched up one of the Russian assault rifles and filled his pockets with spare ammunition magazines. The two

Ukrainian soldiers gathered rations, all the ammunition they could carry, and a pair of Russian military binoculars. There was a small radio in the corner of the room, set upon an upturned wooden crate. Maksim stared thoughtfully.

"This was a Russian OP," Oleksandr guessed. "They would have been in regular contact with their headquarters. As soon as they miss a check-in time, troops will be sent to investigate. We might only have minutes to clear the area…"

They fled the building, trading stealth for speed. Maksim hugged Lyudmila close to him and guided her through the debris.

Once across the shadow-struck access alley, the small group rejoined the three men Maksim had left guarding their retreat and together they ghosted back along the street to where the rest of the refugees had waited fretfully.

"We must get well clear of this area," Maksim addressed the group. He cast a worried glance to the sky. The halo of half-light that presaged dawn was smeared across the horizon, filtered behind a bank of brewing storm clouds. In an hour the sun would rise and they would be cruelly exposed.

He led them south for a block, then west, then finally south again. His relief at being back on course to reach the Shrine to Heroes was tempered by the urgent need to find a place to shelter for the day. The night seemed eerily silent, as though the world was holding its breath. Every small noise seemed amplified, and he walked with his ears strained for the sound of approaching Russian vehicles or the chatter of distant gunfire.

Lyudmila fell back into the knot of refugees. One of the women in the group foraged through her meager possessions and passed her a pair of jeans that were a size too large. Another woman offered her a grey sweater.

McQuade fell in step beside the Ukrainian woman and studied her expression covertly from the corner of his eye. Lyudmila's jaw was thrust forward, her lips pressed into a thin bloodless line. Her gaze remained fixed on the ground ahead of her, unblinking and unwavering. Once, when she shuffled around a fallen tree, she saw McQuade staring at her, but her features remained frozen.

"How is your eye?" he asked quietly.

She shrugged her shoulders as if the injury was irrelevant. "It will heal," she dismissed the question.

"I'm glad you weren't hurt worse…"

"Raped, you mean? You're glad I wasn't raped?" Lyudmila's tone became bitter with accusation.

"I didn't mean that," McQuade defended himself.

"Then what did you mean, American?"

McQuade was spared an answer by Maksim's sudden harshly whispered warning.

"Quiet! Stop!"

The refugees went very still and tensed. They were close to a street corner, pressed against a sidewalk fence and hugging the shadows. Everyone held their breath. Maksim came back to the group, hunched over like he was ducking gunfire.

"There is a Russian armored troop carrier parked in the middle of the road at the intersection ahead of us," he whispered. "There are soldiers on the street. They have set up some kind of a roadblock. It might be that they have discovered their dead comrades back at the observation post and they are searching for us, or perhaps they are conducting an operation to hunt down partisans. We must find a new way south."

McQuade went to the fence and pulled at one of the wooden palings. It came loose in his hand. He pulled harder and the rusted nails holding it in place fell out. He pulled at four more palings until there was a gap in the fence wide enough to pass through. "Here. This way!"

They went through the gap in single file. Oleksandr was at the tail of the column. He replaced the palings, propping them upright against the post and hammering them back in place with the heel of his palm.

They were in the work yard of a motor vehicle repair business. Along the fence line were piled the rusted hulks of wrecked cars, stacked three high. The hulks had been stripped of their parts and were overgrown with tall grass and weeds. At the front of the block stood a factory shed. McQuade approached the building and balanced on his tiptoes to peer through a dusty window. The interior was dark and abandoned. He went to a door and pulled it open quietly. The air smelled of paint fumes and oil.

Maksim stood in the open doorway for a long moment and peered fretfully once more at the sky. The dawn was fast approaching. The shadows had become softer as the new day's light began to spread across the bomb-ravaged city. Dark brooding clouds began to scud across the sky as the stars faded out.

He ducked inside the door and stood for a moment in the heavy silence until his eyes adjusted. The factory was divided into three parts. To his left was a large booth with machinery and compressors. The walls were spattered with a dozen different shades of paint and there were plastic drop sheets hanging draped from steel rails. Ahead of him was a workshop with long shelves against one wall, stacked with motor vehicle parts, windscreens and steel sections of bodywork. Along a wooden workbench were a handful of tools and oily rags. Maksim swept his eyes to the right and saw a small glass-walled cubicle that was the office. He stepped to the doorway and peered inside. He saw a desk littered with grease-stained paperwork, a filing cabinet, and a wall calendar displaying a photograph of a big-breasted blonde woman draped over the hood of a sports car.

Oleksandr and McQuade joined him in the office cubicle's doorway.

"I don't like it," the Ukrainian soldier frowned his concern. "Maksim, we are too close to the Russians. They are at the intersection. If they decide to make a search of the block, we will be discovered."

McQuade shook his head. "We don't have time to find anywhere else," he said. "It's getting light outside. In fifteen minutes, the sun will come up and we'll be caught out in the open. The Russians won't have to search for us – we'll be utterly exposed."

Maksim weighed up both arguments. In truth, he shared Oleksandr's concerns. If the squad of Russian troops searched the area around the intersection, the refugees would surely be discovered. He sighed heavily.

"We have no choice," he conceded. "We must take the chance that the Russians are manning a roadblock and are not a search party."

"You are placing us in great danger," Oleksandr warned. "We are right under the Russian's noses."

"Then we shall have to be quiet," Maksim said, "and trust that God is watching over us. At least," he smiled with masochistic bleakness, "our circumstances cannot be any worse. There is nothing else left to go wrong."

Then it began to rain.

*

They sat in small groups and made desultory conversation while Oleksandr and the other soldier took turns to stand guard. The rain hammered on the iron factory roof, coming in windswept waves. Within the hollow empty shell of the building the sound seemed amplified, noisy as beating drums.

Maksim and McQuade sat on either side of the office desk with a scatter of grease smudge invoices between them. Oleksandr came into the dingy room and dragged a chair to the table. He sat down with a weary sigh and rubbed red-rimmed eyes.

Maxim arched a questioning eyebrow. "Nothing?"

The soldier shook his head. He had just finished four hours of sentry duty, peering out through a dust-smudged window for the first sign of approaching danger. "The street is quiet. The Russians must be huddled inside their APC. Perhaps they don't like the rain," he grunted.

"Good. Let's hope they stay there," Maksim said vehemently and cast a quick glance to the ceiling as if offering up a hasty prayer. A woman came silently into the cubicle carrying Russian military rations, several chunks of crusty bread and small squares of cheese.

"We are still in great danger. The Russians could begin a search at any time," Oleksandr filled his mouth with bread and cheese and spoke through it, chewing noisily.

"We will move again as soon as it is dark," Maksim mollified the soldier. "We will reach the Shrine tonight and be in position to raise the flag of the revolutionaries at dawn tomorrow."

Oleksandr belched loudly and reached for another chunk of bread. "There will be hard fighting and more danger before we reach the Shrine," Oleksandr was the voice of pessimistic caution. "You are counting your chickens, Maksim."

The big man shrugged his shoulders. "Whatever happens is God's will. We place ourselves in His hands. Our cause is righteous. He will protect us."

Oleksandr smirked contemptuously with the cynicism of a professional soldier who knew that guns, not Gods dictated the fortune of war.

McQuade sat listening to the two Ukrainians speak. He reached for a cube of cheese and popped it into his mouth.

"Can I see it?" he asked suddenly.

The two Ukrainians on the far side of the table stopped and looked at the American fighter pilot with sudden wariness.

"See what?" Maksim asked.

"The flag," McQuade said.

"Why?"

"Because I'm risking my life to help you. Because I might die for something I don't even fully understand. Because I want to see what so many Ukrainians just like you two are prepared to die for," his temper flared and his voice rose.

Maksim sat back in his chair and folded his hands across his stomach. He regarded McQuade with shrewd, calculating eyes. "Of course," he said slowly.

The steel case was still cuffed to Oleksandr's wrist. The soldier reached into his boot, unlocked the handcuffs and slid the case across the litter-strewn table. Maksim turned the case until the three locks were facing him. He reached inside the collar of his shirt. On a chain around his neck was a small key. He unfastened the chain and set it down on the desk, then inserted the key into each of the locks. They disengaged with a loud *'click!'*. Maksim lifted the lid of the steel case and took a moment to stare on the contents within. A reverent, almost spiritual expression came over his face. He turned the case slowly and McQuade peered inside.

The ancient flag was wrapped in folds of red cloth. McQuade peeled the material aside and saw a patch of faded blue linen. He looked up at Maksim, puzzled.

The man came around the desk and reached reverently into the box. The flag unfolded as he lifted it free of its dark container. He laid it out carefully on the desk and stood back, hushed.

"I thought it would be silk… or satin," McQuade stared down at the patchwork of cloth. The colors were pale and sun-faded. McQuade could clearly see the hand-stitching that bound the flag's separate panels together. The fringe of the flag was frayed and smudged with small grease-like stains.

"You are gazing at history, American," Maksim's voice was soft with his own awe. "This is the flag of our nation; the original flag of the Ukraine revolutionaries that once united the people of this country against oppression – and soon it will again."

McQuade traced his fingers lightly over the stitching as though he might be able to feel the history the relic was drenched in. He frowned.

"What happens if you succeed, Maksim? What happens if we reach the Shrine and if we raise your revolutionary flag? What happens then?"

Maksim began to carefully fold the flag, his big hands surprisingly dexterous and delicate. Once it was safe inside the steel case and the locks were secured, he let out a long breath and sighed.

"The flag is a gesture, American, and all great efforts begin with a gesture. When we raise the flag, the partisans and the soldiers of our Army will see and know what it represents," Maksim's gaze took on a dreamy hypnotic cast. "They will rally to the flag and word will spread far and wide that the spirit of the revolutionaries still burns in our blood. It will galvanize our resistance against the Russians and reunite us in the common cause of our forefathers. As word spreads about the flag during the days and weeks that follow, so the uprising will gain momentum until, one day, we cast the Russians out of Ukraine and take back our freedom."

*

In the afternoon McQuade took a shift on sentry duty. He went forward to the front of the building and peered out through the small window. The spotted glass was coated in a thin film of dust, strung with cobwebs at each corner. The windowsill was sprinkled with the remains of dead flies.

Beyond the building the street looked still and brooding. Smoke drifted into the sky from a burning house further along the street and the clouds hung low, brimmed full with the threat of more rain.

Light footsteps in the passage behind him caught his attention.

"Lieutenant?"

He turned quickly and saw Lyudmila standing nervous and awkward before him.

"May I speak with you?"

"Yes," he said. She seemed small and fragile in the voluminous sweater, the sleeves rolled up and the jeans hanging baggy off her hips.

"I owe you an apology," she explained. There were high spots of color on her cheeks. "I spoke to Maksim and he told me it was your decision to attack the Russians and rescue me. I judged you harshly and I am sorry for that." She made a small fluttering gesture of apology with her hands and then thrust them deep into the pockets of her jeans, hunching her shoulder and tilting her head to one side as if to see him more clearly.

"Thank you, Lyudmila." He used her name for the first time, sharing her awkwardness. She came a step closer and he caught a whiff of her natural scent. "Are you feeling better?"

"The bruises will heal quickly. The memories not so much," she hung a lopsided humorless smile from her lips. "But at least the memories will not now be nightmares – thanks to your bravery."

McQuade flushed crimson. He felt his cheeks turn scalding hot. He shook his head and stole a glance out through the window to give him a moment to gather his wits. "Ukraine needs you," he said with conviction when he turned back to face her, "and every partisan like you. I couldn't leave you in the hands of the Russians. If this fight isn't about the future of patriots like you, then it's not worth fighting for at all."

She smiled more warmly, disarmed by his words. "I hope that one day I am worthy of the risks you took," Lyudmila said.

Chapter 8:

Late in the afternoon McQuade heard the growl of a big diesel engine and a few minutes afterwards the Russian APC that had been parked at the intersection drove away carrying its cargo of armed soldiers. The refugees gave a collective sigh of relief and began slowly gathering up their few belongings in preparation for the night's journey. The sky was still black with ominous cloud, speeding the onset of darkness.

Maksim came into the mechanical workshop where the refugees had gravitated during the day. He found a stick of chalk on the workbench and went to a wall, his mannerisms suddenly reverting to those of the history professor he had once been.

He spoke to the refugees like they were students and used the wall like a blackboard.

"We are here," he marked the wall and then drew a cross-hatch of several lines, each one representing a city block. "The Shrine to Heroes is here, in the Podil's'syi District," he drew another large box, bordered with shapes to represent buildings and museums on every side. "To reach the Shrine we must follow Mezhova Street past the Lipinka condominium complex and past Boarding School Number Nineteen. Once we reach Lypynka Park we will hide up for the rest of the night. An hour before dawn we will cross the park and make for the Shrine."

Heads nodded mute understanding. The refugees were haggard and sallow-cheeked from endless nights of fatiguing strain. They moved with bovine lethargy towards the rear door of the building and waited patiently while Maksim and Oleksandr went out into the rain-misted gloom.

The two men returned fifteen minutes later. Darkness had draped itself over the city, the new night lit by the glow of fires burning miles away. Maksim's cheeks were flushed from the cold. He rubbed his hands briskly together and then buried them deep in his coat pockets. "We go now," he announced.

*

Every step that carried the refugees nearer to Lypynka Park also brought them closer to danger. The Podil's'syi District had seen heavy fighting in the first days of the war, and the Russians were still on the streets in force.

When the group reached the northern edge of the park, Maksim called a halt to their journey and the refugees crawled into small cover to rest. Some buried themselves in the deep drifts of autumn leaves that carpeted the ground. Others sought the dark shadows for respite. Maksim, McQuade and Oleksandr talked in quiet urgent voices amongst themselves.

Fire engine sirens wailed in the background and a convoy of Russian APCs moved through a distant intersection. The Russian vehicles were fitted with high-powered searchlights that cut and slashed through the darkness.

"We must make it to the far side of the park and then risk a dash across the street," Maksim explained, pointing towards the road where the Russian convoy of armored vehicles patrolled. "The Shrine to Heroes is on the far side of the highway."

"Maksim, the area is crawling with soldiers," McQuade balked.

The Ukrainian nodded, determined. "There is no other way."

The refugees moved off again in single file with Oleksandr leading. The trees in the park stood like skeletal scarecrows. Denuded of their leaves by the change of season they were twisted in grotesque dark shapes, their shadows across the ground sinister and ominous. McQuade walked in the middle of the column with Lyudmila ahead of him, her strides purposeful and impatient.

The parkland folded into gentle hollows and rises. Oleksandr led them on a meandering course, making the most of the terrain's gentle hollows to hide their progress until they were within yards of the highway, spread out behind the shelter of straggly overgrown bushes.

Maksim glanced at his watch and then peered up through the gnarled branches overhead to stare at the sky. He was sweating and breathing hard. He moped his brow with the sleeve of his jacket. The night was still dark, yet in an hour the sun would begin to rise. Somewhere beyond the shattered buildings that marked the eastern skyline he guessed the first pale light of dawn was already beginning to glow. Every minute they waited increased the chances of being discovered.

He crept along the line of bushes, passing on his instructions to the refugees while beyond their tenuous barricade the sounds of diesel engines ebbed and rose as more Russian vehicles traversed the highway.

McQuade peered through the gaps in the foliage and studied the huge grey edifice of the 'Shrine to Heroes' northern building. It looked like a museum with high granite columns across the façade and a vast stone staircase leading up to the front doors. In front of the building, on a broad stretch of paved footpath, were two fountains encircled by what looked to McQuade to be white marble headstones. Each time a Russian APC rumbled along the road their bright search beams played over the huge hulking shape, revealing some new glimpse of detail.

Maksim unfastened the handcuff around his wrist and passed the steel case containing the flag of the revolutionaries to Oleksandr, then gestured to the nearest refugees. They shuffled towards him, crouched low. Their faces were taut and pale with tension. Maksim pointed across the highway.

"Go when I give you the signal," he said. "And keep going. Do not stop for anything. The 'Shrine to Heroes' is at the far end of the plaza. Keep running until you reach it. The rest of us will meet you there." They nodded solemn understanding. There were two middle-aged men and two young women in the group. Maksim crept deeper into the wall of shrubs and studied the highway with the stolen Russian binoculars pressed to his eyes. In the twilight before sunrise they were of little use. He saw the road was clear in both directions and strained his ears for the sound of approaching vehicles. He could hear nothing above the far-away wail of fire engine sirens.

"Go!"

The four refugees sprang from their hiding place and dashed across the highway. They ran cradling their possessions in their arms, bent double and made awkward by their burdens. Their legs were heavy. Their running footsteps making loud slapping sounds on the blacktop that seemed to echo across the fading night. They reached the far side of the highway and without stopping or turning back, disappeared through an open gate beside the museum building.

"Go!"

The next group of refugees were women with children. They reached the far side of the highway safely. A moment later a column of four Russian BMP-2 troop carriers appeared. They rumbled slowly along the highway, searchlights probing the fading shadows. Maksim glanced into the sky with a start of alarm and realized the new day was dawning. Mist drifted through the park; grey snaking tendrils that serpentined between the trees and draped a thin blanket of haze across the highway. The Russian searchlights were diffused and haloed.

The four vehicles reached the far intersection and turned north. The moment they were out of sight, Maksim sent the next group of refugees running across the road with the two Ukraine soldiers in their midst. Soon only he and McQuade remained on the edge of the park.

Maksim peeped through the foliage again and saw the highway was clear in both directions. He seized the sleeve of McQuade's flight suit and dragged him to his feet. "Come on, American!"

The two men burst from the foliage and ran for the verge of the highway. The ground was loose gravel beneath their feet. They hit the blacktop at full stride, McQuade's youth and fitness giving him the edge. The assault rifle banged against his hip as he ran and the heavy weight of the spare ammunition he carried dragged like an anchor. Behind him Maksim ran, pumping his arms furiously, his mouth open, jaw hanging slack. McQuade could hear the harsh grunts of the other man's breath as he strained from the effort.

A Russian APC swerved around the corner suddenly and came surging along the highway, bumping over debris, the diesel engine grinding noisily up through the gears. The commander of the vehicle stood upright in his open hatch, traversing a spotlight. The beam flitted over the mist-wreathed park and then swept across the blacktop.

Maksim froze.

The light of the bright beam trapped the Ukrainian in its glare, standing stranded in the middle of the highway.

"*Stoy!*" The commander of the vehicle shouted an order to halt in Russian. The snarl of the soldier's voice seemed to break the spell that had paralyzed Maksim. He put his head down and ran like the hounds of Hell were at his heels.

McQuade reached the far side of the highway and twisted to glance over his shoulder. He saw Maksim's face, blanched white by his terror. He saw him lit up brightly by the beam of the searchlight. He heard the APC suddenly brake to a halt in the middle of the road and then the fading night was filled with the sounds of soldiers' voices and a stampede of heavy boots.

Maksim reached the far side of the highway and weaved across the sidewalk, dodging the two fountains outside the museum building and angling for the alleyway that passed down the side of the building. McQuade was waiting for the Ukrainian at the open entrance gate.

"Run, you bastard!" the panic infected McQuade. "Don't look back!"

Russian soldiers spilled from the rear of the enemy personnel carrier. One dropped to his knee and fired. The rounds flew wide of Maksim and buried themselves in a nearby stone wall. McQuade peered ahead of him and saw the 'Shrine to Heroes' at the far end of a cobblestoned plaza. The building was pale grey, shrouded in thin veils of morning mist. At the top he saw a bare flagpole.

Between him and the Shrine stretched an open paved courtyard two hundred yards long and maybe a hundred yards wide, bordered on both sides by more buildings. In the middle of the courtyard rose a small waist-high stage. McQuade made a quick calculation and knew for sure they would not make it. The realization made him angry. He slipped the assault rifle off his shoulder and fired at the Russian infantry on the road, sending the enemy troops scrambling for cover.

Maksim slammed into the wall beside him and lunged through the gate. McQuade followed. He looked desperately ahead at the open killing ground that stretched before them. "Keep running!" he urged Maksim on.

They reached the raised stage. A roar of automatic gunfire whiplashed over their heads. McQuade shoved Maksim down behind the platform and heard the Ukrainian scream in sudden agony.

McQuade fired back at the Russians. They were swarming through the gate, not more than a hundred paces behind him. He saw his shots spray wide and high and he cursed bitterly. A groan from Maksim shocked him.

The Ukrainian lay sprawled on the ground, flat on his back. His breathing gurgled in his throat and his jacket was a sodden mess of blood. McQuade stared in despair. He threw down the assault rifle and rolled Maksim gingerly onto his side. The man groaned. His breathing became a heave of short and shallow gasps.

Maksim had been hit by two bullets. One had struck him below the right shoulder blade and the other in the small of his back. Each had torn holes the size of a bottle cap into the pale soft flesh. McQuade gently rolled Maksim over again. He could find no exit wounds.

Maksim was a dead man. It was merely a matter of time.

The Ukrainian professor seemed to sense his life was over.

"I can't breathe," he whispered and a froth of bloody bubbles spilled from the corner of his mouth.

McQuade loosened the man's tie and ripped open the front of his shirt. In the background he heard a rush of stampeding boots. He snatched up the assault rifle, and leaned around the cover of the stage. Two Russian soldiers were dashing towards him, weapons held across their hips while the rest of the squad covered their attack from the sides of the plaza. McQuade fired two short bursts and saw one of the Russians go down hard. The man cried out in pain as he fell and then began screaming in agony, clutching at a groin wound. He rolled onto his side and tucked his knees to his chest, blubbering incoherently in Russian. McQuade fired again and the second Russian was thrown back, struck in the throat from close range. He jerked on the ground and then lay very still.

The rest of the Russians unleashed a fury of firepower in retaliation. McQuade cowered behind the cover of the platform and tucked his head against his chest to make himself a smaller target. Bullets cracked and whined inches above his head.

"You must leave me," McQuade heard Maksim say. "You must go on alone." With blood-slippery fingers the Ukrainian reached for the chain around his neck. "Take the key to the steel case…"

McQuade held out his hand. It was shaking. Staring into the eyes of the dying man, he was surprised by the strength of his regret. He closed his fist around the key and then gripped Maksim's shoulder, suddenly overcome with emotion. "You can still make it," he told the lie in a hoarse whisper.

Maksim smiled benevolently and his eyes dulled. He reached for McQuade's hand and squeezed hard. With a herculean effort he summonsed the last of his strength.

"For as long as the Ukraine flag flies over the 'Shrine to Heroes', the fight for freedom will go on," Maksim croaked. "The flag is a tribute to the generations of patriots who made this country great; a symbol of solidarity and faith eternal. Whilst ever the flag flies in defiance of our oppressors, Ukraine has hope."

McQuade watched the spark of life slowly fade from Maksim's eyes. The Ukrainian freedom fighter drew a last shallow breath and then died with a small sorrowful groan of surrender.

McQuade snatched up the assault rifle and cast a last desolated glance at Maksim's body. The weight of his grief transformed to flames of anger and resolve. He tucked the key safely inside his flight suit and stole a glimpse around the edge of the stage. The Russians were creeping forward, working in pairs with one man covering the advance of another. McQuade leaned out and sprayed the courtyard with bullets and then sprang impulsively to his feet.

One of the Russians lobbed a smoke grenade. It clattered on the cobblestones and rolled like a ball then burst into a billowing grey cloud of haze around the stage. McQuade seized his chance. He broke from cover and dashed towards the Shrine.

The building was a three-story high grey block with windows on every floor, and a wide set of twenty steps rising up to a façade of ornate granite columns. The facing wall of the building was inset with shadowed alcoves, and set into each one was a statue of a heroic figure from Ukraine's past. Atop the building was a waist-high parapet of decorated masonry from where the sudden sound of sporadic gunfire made McQuade look up in shock.

The refugees were leaning over the masonry bulwark, firing down into the plaza. Behind him as he ran, McQuade heard the spatter of their bullets hitting the cobblestones and the sudden sound of a man's agonized groan of pain.

McQuade took the broad steps of the building two-at-a-time and crashed headlong through the open double doors. He slammed against an internal wall, gasping and trembling from fear and exertion. Lyudmila stood in the foyer. She shouldered the huge doors closed and bolted them.

"Where is Maksim?"

"He didn't make it," McQuade doubled over and tried to fill his lungs with air.

"He… he's dead?"

"Yes. The Russians killed him."

The grief and despair made her voice anguished. "Then everything we have risked has all been for nothing?"

"No," McQuade shook his head. He drew himself upright and stared levelly at Lyudmila. He could see the pain and devastation in her eyes. He reached into his flight suit. "Maksim gave me the key to the steel case. He charged me with finishing what he started. I'm going to raise your flag, Lyudmila – but I need help."

*

McQuade stormed up the building's three flights of stairs, his feet pounding on the pavers, and burst out onto the 'Shrine to Heroes' rooftop with Lyudmila close behind him. The refugees turned in startled alarm. McQuade saw Oleksandr leaning against the parapet, the assault rifle kicking in his hands as he fired down into the plaza.

McQuade rushed to the wall and peered down. The Russian squad had reached the stage and were pressing forward. There were four dead bodies sprawled on the ground, each lying in a spreading pool of blood. At the far end of the plaza, more enemy infantry were swarming through the side gate, and the Russians had driven a BMP troop carrier up onto the sidewalk from where its turret-mounted 30mm autocannon could fire.

"Christ!" McQuade swore. He ran to the eastern wall and peered out across the suburbs of Kiev. Dawn was on the horizon; the first golden light of the new day had begun creeping across the world, slowly revealing the utter devastation of a city that had been bombed to rubble and ruin. In the distance, the Dnieper River shone like a dull sheet of beaten copper, reflecting the sunrise.

"Oleksandr! I need the steel case."

"Where is Maksim?"

"He's dead," McQuade said simply. "It's up to us now to raise the flag."

The two men dropped to their knees at the foot of the flagpole. McQuade fumbled with the key. His fingers were sticky with Maksim's blood. He unlocked the steel case and lifted the lid. Oleksandr reached inside and picked up the bundle of linen as though he were holding a baby.

McQuade secured the halyard loop to the top of the flag and then fumbled to secure the bottom corner. He stepped back and Lyudmila wrapped her fingers around a length of halyard and pulled. The flag rose slowly, and at the moment it reached the top of the pole, the sun's rays crested the rim of the horizon and shot the linen through with golden shafts of light. The refugees stopped firing down at the Russians and turned, hushed and made breathless with a spiritual kind of awe. One of the women began to weep quietly. Oleksandr stood stiffly to attention and saluted. Lyudmila tied the halyard off and shuffled close to McQuade. Her voice was muted and small with emotion.

"It is done. Thank you," she said softly.

Then the rumble of heavy engines carried on the morning air, and McQuade went to the parapet to see that the effort had all been in vain. The sacrifices, the risks, the terrible cost in lives had been for nothing.

Because a Russian column of armored personnel carriers was coming to steal the miracle of hope away, and to drench the 'Shrine to Heroes' granite walls in fresh blood.

Chapter 9:

Six Russian troop carriers came into the sunrise and blocked off the highway in both directions, trapping the refugees. McQuade saw infantry spilling from the rear doors of each vehicle and knew there were too many of the enemy and too much firepower arrayed against him to hold out for more than a few minutes. He glanced sideways at Lyudmila and Oleksandr, the hopelessness of their situation written on his face.

There was nothing helpful that could be offered by either of them. They must simply fight to the end; until there was no one left standing and no ammunition left to fire. Oleksandr's face hardened with the fatalistic resolve of a soldier. He would take as many of the loathsome Russian bastards with him as he could and, one day when the history of this war was told, his compatriots would re-tell the story about this bloody battle and cuff away tears of patriotic pride.

"Everyone hold your fire until the Russian infantry are inside the confines of the plaza," McQuade ordered the refugees. He could see the fear on their faces as they turned to him, and he was sure his own expression reflected their dread. In just a few furious minutes they would all be dead.

He would conserve their ammunition until the Russians attempted to storm the building, turning the cobblestones red with blood. The Russians, he was sure, would advance under the covering fire of their APCs and behind a choking wall of smoke.

"If we surrender, we'll all be killed," McQuade felt compelled to explain to Lyudmila why he was planning to fight against such impossible odds.

"Of course. Surrender is not an option for any of us. We all knew this moment would come."

"You never expected to escape once the flag was raised?"

"No. But we have faith."

"In your God?"

"Yes, and in the patriotism of our brothers and sisters fighting the same war with the same passion."

McQuade smiled wryly and looked over his shoulder at the sweeping view of the grey ravaged city. Fires were still burning and columns of thick smoke climbed into the sky. To the east the morning was lit by the flashing glow of far-away Russian artillery. "Well pray for a miracle, and pray it happens soon," he indulged her, but smiled despite his cynicism. "And let's hope your God is listening."

Down on the highway the Russian infantry were organizing into squads and the APCs were moving into position on the footpath, each vehicle bringing its autocannon to bear on the 'Shrine to Heroes' building. McQuade slipped the assault rifle off his shoulder, checked he had a full magazine of ammunition, then went to stand beneath the flagpole.

He cleared his throat and heads turned in his direction.

"Maksim told me I was a selfish, hollow man who cared about nothing but myself," McQuade said to the refugees lining the parapet. "He was right. But I want you all to know that your bravery and your patriotism have inspired me. I'm proud to be here with you."

The refugees recognized the American pilot's confession for what it was and they warmed to him and smiled. Their cheer turned into a shout of defiance against the Russians.

McQuade joined the rest of the refugees at the parapet in time to see the first enemy infantry rush through the sidewalk gate and into the plaza. When they reached the stage in the center of the cobblestones, McQuade knew, the next squad of troops would surge forward until the Russians were charging in endless waves.

"Wait until they get beyond the cover of the stage," McQuade pulled the assault rifle to his shoulder and sighted on a Russian soldier who was coming forward with bold strides.

The Russians were skilled and patient. Once inside the confines of the cobblestoned courtyard they fanned out. The refugees had the benefit of height and cover – but it would be only fleeting. When the shooting started the enemy would dash forward and be across the killing ground in just a few furious seconds.

The Russian Platoon commander leading the first assault put a whistle to his lips and blew a single shrill note. The first line of soldiers gave a loud roar and surged forward, firing from the hip to cover their advance.

McQuade seized Lyudmila by the shoulder. "Take the women and children and escape before it's too late," he urged her. "You can still flee. There must be an exit from this building that would lead you further south. Go now, before the Russians cordon off the entire precinct."

"No," her face was flushed, her eyes glittering with fear and breathless recklessness. "I'm staying. We're all staying."

McQuade sighted on the Russian officer with the whistle to his lips. The first squad of enemy soldiers swept around either side of the stage and then rejoined, bunching towards the center of the plaza as they dashed for the steps that lead up to the front double-doors. The refugees hunched over their motley collection of weapons and held their breath. As they ran forward, two Russians threw smoke grenades and a curtain of cloud began to billow, filling the courtyard with swirling grey haze.

"Now! Open fire!"

The refugees fired – not as a well-drilled unit – but in a ragged cough of smoke and noise, the weapons kicking against their shoulders. The sound was like the spatter of gravel thrown against a window. One Russian was shot in the foot and stumbled to the ground, screaming and gushing blood. Another was struck in the side of the face as he turned his head to shout to his comrades. The bullet turned his flesh to rubber for a split-second, deforming his head so that it seemed to swell. The impact snapped him backwards and he dropped to the ground, already dead. His helmet spun from the pulped bloody flesh of his ruined face and went rolling across the ground. Two more Russians went down in the initial fusillade clutching bloody wounds. One man was shot in the lower abdomen. He rolled onto his stomach and tried to crawl to shelter, moving like a maimed caterpillar and leaving a bright red smear of blood in his trail.

McQuade fired a short burst of bullets at the Russian officer. He missed. He cursed bitterly, adjusted his aim and fired again. The officer folded at the knees and sagged slowly to the ground clutching his hip. McQuade changed aim and fired at two soldiers who had reached the steps rising up to the front doors. He was shooting almost directly down on them. He missed both Russians but a woman refugee further along the parapet dropped a grenade. The explosion eviscerated both Russians so that all that remained of them were pieces of butchered bloody debris.

Three more Russians fell to the cobblestones and then the autocannons mounted in the turrets of the Russian APCs opened fire.

The roar of the 30mm weapons was a deafening, chattering nightmare. The huge shells blasted the building's masonry façade and tore splinters from the railing. The refugees ducked instinctively and cowered behind their cover, white faced and suddenly terrified. McQuade crawled along the line until he reached two middle-aged men. They were dressed in the work clothes of farmers or mechanics. They were round-shouldered and heavy in the gut with the ruddy complexions of laboring folk who worked with their hands.

"Ground floor!" McQuade snapped. "Pile everything you can find up against the front doors. We have to barricade the entrance. Tables, chairs, filing cabinets. Everything you can find. Go!"

The relentless hammer blows of Russian autocannon fire continued to pepper the parapet, kicking up stonework fragments and forcing the refugees to cower. In his mind's eye McQuade saw the Russians in the courtyard scrambling up the steps to the building. Soon they would be throwing grenades through shattered windows. Once the front doors were battered down, the fight would be over in a matter of just minutes.

He looked up at the linen flag of the revolutionaries waving in the breeze, the fabric so threadbare with age that it was almost translucent. As he stared, a Russian bullet plucked a hole in the material.

He heard Lyudmila give a loud shout and he turned, terrified that she had been shot.

"Look!" she had her head raised above the rim of the parapet, careless of the hammering autocannons that flailed and thrashed the stonework.

McQuade took a deep breath and poked his head over the top of the bulwark. He frowned. Nothing made sense. The park beyond the highway was wreathed in thick rolling clouds of smoke, and he could see dark shadows moving within the haze. A brilliant flash of light flared in the gloom and a split-second later one of the Russian BMP-2s exploded in a fireball.

"Christ!"

"The flag!" Lyudmila's face split into a giddy smile. "Ukraine's patriots are rallying to our fight for freedom."

In response to the attack in their rear, the Russian armored vehicles turned their fire on the danger approaching from the park. The assault across the plaza wavered. For a moment the infantry faltered and McQuade saw a glimmer of hope.

"Fire!" he bellowed.

The refugees rose from their shelter and aimed down into the courtyard. The Russian infantry, cruelly exposed in the open and without the support of the heavy machine guns aboard the APCs, edged backwards.

"Keep firing!" McQuade urged the refugees on. "Kill the bastards!"

"Ukraine!" Oleksandr cried, his blood-lust inflamed by the fury of battle.

"Ukraine!" the rest of the refugees took up the gallant cry, their throats parched, their mouths dry.

One of the men McQuade had sent downstairs to barricade the double-doors came staggering and breathless to the rooftop. His face was shiny with sweat.

"The partisans are here!" he declared.

"Yes," McQuade nodded. "They're attacking through the park. They just destroyed one of the enemy's troop carriers."

"No," the man shook his head and his face lit like the sunrise. He dashed across to the southern face of the building and leaned far out over the lip of the parapet. "The partisans!"

McQuade and Lyudmila turned and stared in wonder. Three bomb-ravaged blocks away but coming closer with every second was a ragged convoy of farm trucks, four-wheel drives and battered family sedans crammed with rebel Ukraine fighters.

Lyudmila squealed with delight and impulsively hugged McQuade, her eyes bright and alive. "You asked for a miracle, American," her smile beamed. "God has delivered."

*

The leader of the partisans was an unshaven brute of a man named Borysko. He stared at McQuade's flight suit and eyed him warily as Lyudmila relayed the events of the past few days and explained McQuade's plight. The partisan rubbed his stubbled chin. He smelled of sweat and tobacco. There were bloodstains down the front of his rumpled shirt and his hands were bruised and calloused.

"We promised we would give him safe passage back to his army," Lyudmila finished pleading her case. "Maksim gave his word."

Borysko grunted. He paced around the rooftop, his eyes narrowed and assessing. The Russian infantry had retreated from the plaza, leaving thirty bloody corpses in their wake, and had turned to do battle with the unit of Ukraine soldiers attacking through the park. Borysko stared up at the flag of the revolutionaries for a long time.

"We can hold here for a month, maybe longer," he declared. "Now that word is spreading about the flag, by the end of the day we will have a thousand armed men to defend this place. I think I can spare one of them to escort you west, American."

*

The vehicle was a battered Lada four-wheel drive Niva, and the driver was a wiry dark-haired partisan who chain-smoked cigarettes and carried a knife tucked inside the belt of his pants. He had olive oily skin and dark suspicious eyes.

"The Ukraine Army is massing west of the city," Lyudmila explained to McQuade when they were standing at the southern exit of the building. "Borysko says that once the Russians have beaten off the attack in the park, they will call for reinforcements and your escape route will be cut off."

She thrust out her hand suddenly and McQuade took it. Her grip was firm. "Thank you for all you did," she said stiffly.

McQuade smiled. "I'll be coming back," he vowed. "One day, I'll return here."

Lyudmila nodded. "We will have a meal together and celebrate the end of the war."

"Yes," McQuade held her hand. "It's a dinner date."

Two hours later the driver braked at the side of a deserted stretch of road and four armed Ukraine scouts wearing ghillie camouflage suits emerged from a clump of overgrown bushes. The driver lit a cigarette. "This is as far as I take you, American," the man said. "The Ukraine Army is encamped two miles further west. These soldiers will escort you the rest of the way. You can relax now. Your ordeal is over."

LUTSK AIR BASE
WESTERN UKRAINE

Chapter 10:

He stepped out of the Humvee and cast his eyes into the sky, blinking against the dazzling colors of sunset. The driver came around the vehicle and handed him his bag. McQuade nodded his gratitude. The Humvee sped away and left him standing there, disorientated by the changes that had occurred during the few days he had been hospitalized in Germany.

A row of temporary hangars had been erected at the end of the airstrip, and he could see at least a dozen new demountable buildings, all of them neatly arranged with military precision around a network of worn walking paths. There were more fighters too, and more noise. Lutsk Air Base had transformed – seemingly overnight – into a hub of bustling, urgent military activity.

He walked slowly towards the nearest building. His eyes were downcast and he frowned in thought. He was gaunt, his skin pale and shadowed blue by new-shaved beard. He had lost weight in the last few days so that his uniform seemed to hang from the frame of his shoulders. His eyes were dark and smudged by deep shades of fatigue as they took in all the changes that had taken place in his absence.

Servicemen, mechanics and administration staff scurried in all directions around him. Arc lights came on around the base as the sun sank below the horizon. McQuade reached the steps of a demountable. He could hear an air conditioner rattling. He reached for the railing to take the first step and then stopped suddenly. Some instinct had made him hesitate. He turned and lifted his eyes.

For many seconds neither of them moved. McQuade stood with his shoulders bunched and his chin raised in a silent defiant challenge.

Ron Hernandez arched his eyebrows in recognition and then a slow satisfied smile tugged at one corner of his mouth.

"When I heard the news that you wanted to come back downrange, I didn't believe it," Hernandez came across the patch of worn grass with his hand extended, his smile broadening. "I thought you would have been on the first C-17 back to the States."

McQuade shook hands. "I have some unfinished business here."

Hernandez nodded and his expression became thoughtful. "I called Landstuhl Regional Medical Center every day to check on your progress. The German receptionist said you were giving the nurses hell."

McQuade didn't smile. Hernandez sensed his wingman was somehow different; changed by his ordeal. He was more somber – as though he had aged overnight.

"They treated me for dehydration and a few bumps and cuts. It wasn't worth a hospital stay. I could have flown again the next day."

"I think the medical term is an overabundance of caution," Hernandez said dryly.

"It was that and more," McQuade said. "Once I got back through the lines, I was surrounded by a team of Army doctors. They turned me into a pin cushion and hooked me up to an IV to get fluids into me. Then I went fifteen rounds with USAF intelligence officers. They wanted to debrief me to see if I'd learned anything about the Russian occupation, their tactics, and the Ukraine resistance movement. That experience was more arduous than evading the Russians."

Hernandez laughed politely, but behind the façade of his expression his eyes were analyzing and assessing McQuade's temperament. The young pilot *was* different; more subdued, more… *what?*

"Lieutenant Colonel Thille visited before I was flown to Germany, and so did the chaplain."

"The chaplain?" Hernandez's surprise was genuine. "Did he splash you with Holy Water and perform an exorcism?"

"Not quite," McQuade smiled, but it looked more like a wince. "I've never been a believer… but being trapped behind enemy lines changes your perspective on life, you know? It changed me, in more ways than I care to admit."

"In good ways?"

McQuade made a self-deprecating gesture with his hands and looked apologetic and humbled. "A few days ago, I stood on the tarmac and told you I didn't know any Ukrainians and that I signed on to fight for America, not foreigners. I was an ass. I know that now. You told me that Uncle Sam had spent millions of dollars training me to fly a Viper and not a single cent on teaching me humility. Remember?"

"Yeah," Hernandez said. "I remember."

"Well, I learned that lesson in the mud and the blood of Kiev. I learned what heroism looks like and what true sacrifice means. I learned that people are people, no matter what part of the world they live in, and that they want the same things that Americans do; freedom – freedom to choose how they live, where they work, who they love and who fucking governs them," his voice filled with savage passion. "That's why I wanted to return to duty. I've got a job to do, and it's an important job – because people who can't defend themselves and who have lost all hope are relying on us to fight the battle on their behalf."

Hernandez's smile warmed. "Then you've come to the right place and at exactly the right time. There's a major operation in the planning. Word is we're flying tomorrow at dawn to hit the Russians hard. Why don't you check in and I'll meet you in the mess tent after you get settled? The first beer is on me. You look like a man in need of a quiet drink."

*

McQuade was not tired; his brain was overactive with apprehension and dread for the morning's mission. He lay in his narrow bunk, listening to the sounds of truck engines revving, and it was past midnight before he finally drifted off. When he woke, he was screaming with the blackness and the terror of the collapsed factory tunnel upon him again. He stumbled out of bed and kicked his shin against a chair. He felt like he was suffocating. He needed fresh air and light.

He flung the door open and bright arc lights atop guard towers flared in his eyes. He gulped down air like a desperate drowning man. His gasping panic slowed. He licked dry cracked lips. Beneath his t-shirt he could feel his heart pounding against the cage of his ribs. On the far side of the camp, his back against a high fence, a bored sentry stared at him curiously.

McQuade went back inside and turned on the lights. There was a stack of well-thumbed magazines on a table. He picked one at random and carried it to his bunk, forcing himself to read until the alarm by his elbow began its strident buzzing.

It was 03:30. There was a briefing in thirty minutes.

McQuade showered and quickly shaved then returned to his small room and stared into the locker against the far wall. Two new flight suits hung from hangers. He chose the first one and put his patches in their proper places, then tightened the Velcro cuffs at his wrists. He moved like an old man. His body ached and his eyes felt filled with grit. He laced up his combat boots, shrugging off the stiffness and the flutter of butterflies in his guts with his jaw clenched, his attitude grimly determined.

As 04:00 approached, the eight pilots flying the sortie began to file into the briefing room. The mission was a high-altitude bombing attack on a complex of buildings in the Holosiivs'kyi district on the southern outskirts of Kiev that were being used by Russian military command.

"Alright everyone, grab a coffee and a briefing materials packet from the table," the Mission Commander said in a loud voice as the pilots shuffled around in the cramped space. "Find a place and get settled."

McQuade picked up an envelope from the table and spotted Hernandez sitting in the first chair of the front row. He walked across the room to join him. McQuade reached inside the envelope and pulled out two maps, a lineup card, an attack card and a high-resolution satellite photo showing the building complex that was the target for the raid.

He studied the image carefully. The complex was a knot of four low-rise buildings set on a square plot of grassy ground, surrounded by a network of roads and intersections. On the eastern side of the complex were two open-air parking lots and further east was the dark snaking line of the Dnieper River. Each building on the photo had been labelled and numbered. Around the edges of the satellite photo were computer time stamps, longitude and latitude readouts and official USAF image identification numbers.

The eight Vipers were broken into two flights of four. Hernandez's flight was call sign 'Hammer'.

The briefing began on time with a roll-call and then an officer from the base's weather shop stepped in front of the gathering. An overhead projector displayed a satellite photo on northern Ukraine against a white wall. Much of Kiev lay under a blanket of smoke and cloud.

"The ceiling over the target is two thousand feet, partial obscure, but winds are expected to pick up over the next few hours, sweeping down from the north of the continent," the officer gestured. "The chances the cloud and smoke will have thinned significantly by the time you reach the target are good. Our forecast is for no ceiling, but limited visibility of five or maybe six nautical miles. But this is weather analysis we're talking about; it's fifty percent guesswork and fifty percent PFM."

PFM was military aviator speak for 'pure fucking magic'.

A Major from Intel followed the officer from the weather shop. The satellite image on the overhead projector was replaced with a map depicting the mission's IP-to-target route and also an egress route that led away to the south.

"The map explains it all," the Major was a dry, dusty man with pale skin and a mouth that barely moved when he spoke. His tone was fussy and precise; the voice of an officer who had spent the bulk of his career behind a desk.

"As you can see, you'll approach the target on a zero-nine-three-degree heading. Your IP is the center of the Druzhby Street Bridge over the Ros' River in the city of Bila Tserkva, south of Kiev. This is a good place to get your final nav update before you pick up a new heading of zero-zero-five-degrees, following the road north towards your target. SA-8 sites are expected here, and here, as you approach the outskirts of Kiev," he pointed to the map, identifying two locations. "And we've identified two other SAM sites – type unknown – on the outskirts of Vasylkiv," he pointed again to identify the city on the map. Vasylkiv was about twenty clicks south of Kiev and five miles east of their approach route.

The Major paused for a moment to allow the pilots to absorb the information before he went on, his voice dry as old parchment. "Once you are on target, I recommend coming off right once you drop your bombs. We believe following the banks of the Dnieper River is your best way to the egress point in order to avoid the inner city concentrations of SA-7s, SA-8s and SA-21 Growlers."

There was a moment of taut silence. The Major suddenly paused and seemed to be choosing his words carefully, delicately avoiding McQuade's eyes when he finally spoke again.

"If anyone is unfortunate enough to be shot down, Intel recommends your E and E plan should be to make for the river and follow it south, away from the city until a pickup can be arranged. The code word for the day is 'Bluegrass', the number of the day is sixty-six, and the letter today is Z for zulu. Memorize them all – and remember to review your ISOPREP card. If Search and Rescue needs to identify you in a hurry, any of these codes will confirm you are an American pilot. Are there any questions?"

A pilot seated directly behind McQuade asked a question about the range of the Russian SA-21 Growlers and then the Lieutenant Colonel commanding the mission stepped back in front of the assembly.

"Our objectives for today's mission are simple. We must destroy the target. Intel believes it is a major command headquarters for the Russian Army currently besieging Kiev. Decapitating the enemy's command structure will go a long way to loosening the noose around the city's neck. We must meet our delivery parameters, maintain a status of mutual support... and we must all get home safely. Our secondary objectives are no frag and no mortalities."

The commander glanced at the faces of the assembled pilots and saw their stern, focused expressions. He nodded. "Very well. Now here is the bad news – your weapons package will each be two MK-84 two-thousand-pound bombs." He held up his hands to ward off the groans and muttered discontent from the assembled pilots and raised his voice, putting steel into his words. But beneath his brusque explanation was a sense of his own bitter frustration. "I know. I know. It's thirty-year-old technology. Dumb bombs were phased out years ago, but the fact is that we're in a war, people. Right now, the pilots flying ops across Poland, Germany and the Baltics are getting all the munitions they need and we're getting whatever can be shipped across the Atlantic. Command tells me there are problems with some of the GPS chips in the JDAM kits coming into theater. There's no point belly-aching about it. It's old-school, but old school worked just fine during Desert Storm. So suck it up, people. We fight with what we've got." He concluded the briefing by rattling off step time, engine start time and taxi time, then cast one long last glance around the room at the assembled pilots. "Takeoff is scheduled for 05:50 zulu. Is there anything requiring explanation?"

No one spoke.

McQuade and the rest of the pilots filled the details into their lineup cards then added the Have Quick frequencies and their Mode squawks.

The Lieutenant Colonel had a final point to make. "Joker for this mission is 7.0 and Bingo is 6.5." Bingo fuel was the lowest amount of fuel the fighters could carry over the target and still make it safely back to an Allied air base. Joker fuel was traditionally set at five hundred pounds above Bingo. Joker was like the orange fuel-empty icon suddenly glowing on the dashboard of a passenger car. It was a warning.

The rest of the briefing covered the technical details of the mission including takeoff spacing, cruise speed, the air-refueling plan and altitude.

The meeting was about to break up when the base commander unexpectedly appeared in the doorway. He made eye contact with the Lieutenant Colonel and came into the room, his brow deeply furrowed, his expression dark and troubled.

Someone called a brisk, "Attention!" and the pilots sprang to their feet. The Colonel waved the men back to their seats with a brusque, "As you were."

For several long seconds he stood silently before the pilots, marshaling his thoughts. When he spoke at last, his tone was somber. "I'm sorry for the interruption, but I have some additional intel. Moments before this briefing began," he said gravely, "we learned from 'Borderless Aid Worldwide' that the Russians in Kiev have created 'kill squads' with the sole mission of hunting down local Ukrainian citizens inside the city suspected of insurgency. The 'kill squads' are executing suspects in the streets."

McQuade's head snapped up from his lineup card. 'Borderless Aid Worldwide' was a well-known humanitarian organization that was active across the European battlefront. Its members offered urgent medical attention and food supply support to refugees.

"Quite simply, the Russians appear to be committing atrocities on par with the ruthless Nazi slaughter of innocents we saw during the Second World War. These obscene 'kill squads' are reportedly roaming the length and breadth of the city, killing indiscriminately and without reason. We believe the campaign has been initiated by the new military commander appointed to the Ukraine theater. He, or his minions, might well be operating from those very same buildings you are tasked with destroying today. A successful attack might not only aid the remnants of the Ukraine Army still fighting in the city, it might make the Russians rethink their brutal reign of slaughter. Do a good job."

The somber pilots left to brief within their own flights. A crew van was waiting to transport 'Hammer' flight to the briefing demountable across from the squadron's life-support shop.

It was still dark when the pilots emerged into the night. The air smelled of smoke and diesel fumes. The stars in the sky were blotted out behind smudges of cloud. McQuade pulled the collar of his flight suit close around his neck and shivered involuntarily. Tiny insects of apprehension crawled across his skin.

When they arrived at the squadron briefing trailer, Hernandez went back over the specifics of the mission, detailing tanker ops and formation discipline. The pilots were tense, their faces drawn. All of them understood the perils the mission would present.

"We've all trained for this. None of us are rookies. We know what to expect and we know we can deal with anything the Russians throw at us," Hernandez stressed. "And besides…" he tried a little levity to alleviate the crackling tension, "it still beats flying heavies and delivering rubber dog shit to Hong Kong."

They walked as a group to the life support trailer and began the ritual of preparing themselves for combat. McQuade removed each patch from his flight suit and bagged them, then checked he had his combat wallet tucked into his back pocket that held his dog tags, his ID and a twenty-dollar bill. He stepped into his G-suit and zipped it up. Then he reached for his survival vest – and paused. His fingers were trembling and his heart seemed to skip a beat. He could feel cold clammy sweat on the palms of his hands. From the far corner of the room Ron Hernandez watched the young pilot fight the demons of his doubts.

With a sudden impulsive snatch, McQuade reached for the vest and shrugged it on.

He took a deep breath and swung his arms. The G-suit gripped tightly, the vest cinched across his chest. He felt like he was wearing a stranger's skin. To distract himself he checked out a 9mm M9 Beretta from the weapons locker and loaded it.

Ron Hernandez cleared his throat suddenly and McQuade wheeled on his heel. The other three pilots of 'Hammer' flight were standing in a knot at the far end of the cramped space. Hernandez had his hands behind his back. He was smiling.

"We've got something for you," he said to McQuade. "Everyone in the squadron contributed, so it's a group effort. The life support guys used one of your old helmets to get the fit right."

From behind his back he produced a helmet. It was painted bright red with a design of white lightning bolts and blue stars. Across the top of the visor was the word, 'Vader'.

"We got together once we heard you were coming back and the CO shared with us the details of your survival story and that hero stunt you performed with the Ukrainian flag. We decided 'Lone Wolf' no longer suited you as a callsign. So, from today onwards, you are callsign, 'Vader'."

McQuade reached out for the new helmet, surprised, touched and excruciated with embarrassment by the gesture. He was unaccustomed to the generosity of others and was unsure how to react. He turned the helmet over in his hands, admiring the design and then ran his fingertips across the white lettering.

"Why 'Vader'?"

Hernandez smiled again. "Don't you know your *Star Wars*, man? Darth Vader is the ultimate redeemed villain; it fits you perfectly. When you arrived here, I thought you were a cocky asshole who didn't care about anyone but himself. But then we heard about everything you did to help those Ukrainian refugees and the stunt you pulled to raise that flag. You turned out all right, McQuade."

*

With the pilots in their cockpits and all pre-flight checks completed, Hernandez began the check-in and everyone answered in order. The Vipers began to taxi. McQuade twirled his finger in the air to signal that he was ready. His crew chief waved him forward and snapped off a salute. McQuade saluted back. He was trembling; already a sheen of sweat glistened his brow. He took half a dozen deep breaths and coaxed his fighter towards the arming area.

As the Vipers passed the control tower McQuade could see small knots of ground crew and bystanders gathered to watch the takeoff. He reached the arming area and set his brakes while he waited for the arming crews to inspect his jet. He thrust both hands up into the air, signaling to the crew on the ground that it was safe to crawl beneath the fighter. While he waited for the lead crew chief to give him the thumbs-up, McQuade ran his eyes over the cockpit controls for the hundredth time.

The lead crew chief signaled and saluted. McQuade turned on his ECM pod and armed his ejection seat.

Hernandez released his brakes and his Viper went racing along the runway, engine roaring as it lifted into the dawn sky. McQuade made sure the master arm switch was set to 'Simulate', and then released his brakes. The F-16 flashed down the runway like a thoroughbred.

Outside McQuade's cockpit the first delicate light of the new day was rimming the horizon, pale and watery behind a foreboding smudge of dark clouds and a scar of smoke.

*

The Vipers leveled off at twenty-two thousand feet, maintaining radio silence as they flew towards Kiev. The air-refueling proceeded without incident and then the two four ship flights turned their attention to reaching the IP and the subsequent attack.

Hernandez contacted the airborne AWACS that was controlling the mission by providing clearance into the combat zone and warning of Russian air threats.

"Magoo, Hammer One," McQuade overheard Hernandez's conversation with the AWACS.

"Hammer One, you are five by five," the controller replied. "Magoo authenticates alpha-xray."

"Hammer One authenticates delta-zulu."

Quickly Hernandez asked for an update, called a PUC (Pilot Update Code). The controller aboard the AWACS sounded young and irritatingly enthusiastic. "All players are on board. Picture to target is free of air threats."

"Roger, Magoo."

It was the final clearance. Hernandez keyed his mike. "Hammer Flight Fence in! Master arm on, check ECM pod on. Chaff and flares on!" His voice became edged with tension as the Vipers crossed into hostile territory.

The F-16s raced east and reached the IP over the Ros' River at Bila Tserkva, then changed course smoothly for the final run to target. McQuade was a lather of sweat inside his flight suit. He heard himself gasping for breath inside his face mask.

He scanned his cockpit controls to distract himself, then checked his RWR. With the target off his nose, he flicked his master arm switch to 'Arm'.

The radio in McQuade's cockpit suddenly filled with the static of Russian jamming devices. Hernandez's voice came crackling in McQuade's ears.

"Hammer, push 'active'," Hernandez instructed, initiating each aircraft's Have Quick anti-jam mode.

McQuade hung his head to the side and peered down at the world.

Twenty-two thousand feet below him, the road to Kiev twisted like a dying python across the landscape, surrounded by patches of bare brown ground and clumps of dense forest. Here and there McQuade could make out secondary roads that ran like arteries from the highway towards farms and small villages. The cloud was breaking up, the smoke shredding.

A sudden cry of alarm loud in his headset startled him.

"Hammer One has multiple missile launches!"

Another pilot in the flight added to the alert. "SAMs right, two o'clock!"

McQuade saw the wicked menaces as they rose through the thinning cloud trailing grey tails of vapor, and had to clamp down on the sudden spike of fear. There was no way a SA-8 missile could reach the Vipers at their current altitude. But it was a warning; the Russians would be expecting them.

McQuade kept his finger hovering over the chaff dispenser trigger as a precaution. The seconds seemed to drag by, each one a new excruciating torture of fear and apprehension. He could hear his breath catch with each exhalation.

On his HUD he saw they were ten miles from the target and he turned all his attention to the task of dropping his bombs, grateful for the distraction from the SAM-filled sky.

He concentrated on the CCRP steering line in the center of the HUD and coaxed the TD box over the target, waiting for the distance to count down to a release while he continued to finesse the stick. The TD box wavered then realigned. The 'max-toss' cue appeared and seemed to glow on his display.

Wait! Wait! He counted down the seconds, feeling his apprehension rise. He imagined one of the Russian SAMs rising up from the ground, punching through the cloud bank and climbing after him. He started to fight for every lungful of air as panic squeezed his chest. The urge to release his bombs early and flee was almost irresistible.

Wait!

Finally, the solution cue passed through the flight-path marker and the indicators on the HUD merged at a single point. He hit the pickle button. The two huge bombs released with a loud *'clunk'* and McQuade hooked hard to the right and made for the egress point.

He pushed the power up and caught up with Hernandez. The remaining two Vipers rejoined the formation sixty seconds later and the fighters sprinted west to clear the combat zone.

McQuade slumped back in the Viper's reclined seat and felt a wave of relief wash over him. A muscle in his cheek began to jerk. His whole face was clammy with sweat, and his arms and legs felt rubbery.

The Vipers reached the edge of the combat area and checked out with the circling AWACS. Thirty minutes later McQuade rolled out on final and spotted Lutsk runway.

He had won; he had conquered his fear and re-discovered his courage.

Chapter 11:

After the mission debrief, the pilots went to the base mess tent to catch up on news of the war. McQuade sat quietly watching a flat-screen TV as a CMM news anchor began detailing the spate of recent terrorist bomb attacks that had rocked Berlin. Hernandez stood surrounded by some of the squadron's other pilots who were anxious to hear about the mission. Snatches of the conversation carried across the vast tent space to where McQuade sat.

Finally Hernandez broke away from the other pilots and set a mug of coffee down on the table beside McQuade. "You okay, Vader?"

"Yeah," McQuade clawed his hands through his hair and smiled. He was physically exhausted and emotionally drained.

"Are you hanging around for a few hours?"

"No. I need to sleep. There was a slot on the squadron's schedule for alert duty alongside you this afternoon. I volunteered."

Pilots were rarely thrilled to see their name of the alert duty schedule that rotated in eight-hour shifts around the clock; it was all but guaranteed to be a tedious waste of time. Since arriving in-country the squadron had not yet scrambled to a single air defense threat.

Hernandez looked bewildered. "I thought you would be sick of flying on my wing."

McQuade avoided a direct answer but there was grim resolve in his words when he replied. "I've missed a lot of fighting," he explained. "I need to be back in the air flying."

*

The war was going badly for the Allies.

In Poland, thousands of NATO troops fighting to defend Warsaw had surrendered to the Russians while the shattered remnants of the Army fled west towards Germany, or north towards the port of Gdansk. In the Baltic States the Russians were tightening their grip on insurgents and partisans. And in

Ukraine, Russian tanks had crashed across the Belarus southern border, opening up a second front to pound the troops defending the city of Kiev into submission.

The story elsewhere around the world was similar. In the Pacific, the Chinese were sweeping through the South China Sea and pressuring the American Pacific Fleet while their fighter jets and armies rampaged through Asia.

McQuade scanned the bleak news headlines on his iPad, and his thoughts drifted to the handful of freedom fighters he had left behind in the bomb-ruined streets of Kiev. He wondered whether they still fought on, or whether they had been crushed under the steel tracks of the advancing Russian assault.

The sudden clamor of the klaxon on the wall of the base's alert shack was so unexpected that for long seconds he and Ron Hernandez stared at the blinking red light with expressions of utter bewilderment. Then the realization struck them. McQuade was overcome with wild elation and alarm.

Scramble!

The two pilots sprang from their chairs and sprinted out through the door towards the hangar where their fighters waited. The afternoon sky was tinted with a haze of high cloud, the sun still high in the sky. The air smelled of smoke and aviation fuel.

When they reached the darkened gloom of the hangar, one of the base intelligence officers was waiting for them. His face was flushed, and he was gasping like a bellows. His uniform was sweat-stained. He sucked in a deep breath and blurted in a rush, "Russian Bear bombers over Kiev. They're pounding on Ukrainian positions. Command wants you to hit the fuckers hard," he scraped his hand across his brow, bent over at the waist and propped his hands on his knees, still breathing like a marathon runner at the end of a race. "Contact AWACS when you're airborne for details."

The pilots on alert were expected to have their fighters in the air within five minutes of the klaxon sounding, and endless hours of thought and planning had gone into the streamlined process.

The pilots and maintenance officers prepared each fighter for alert by completing all the necessary pre-flight checks, pre-aligning the Viper's internal navigation systems and setting up their personal gear in the cockpits at the start of each shift.

Hernandez and McQuade were already fully dressed with their G-suits and parachute harnesses hanging from pegs on the boarding ladders attached to the side of their waiting fighter, and their helmets already connected to the F-16's oxygen system and perched on the side of the cockpit.

The two pilots separated and ran to their aircraft.

Each Viper carried a full complement of air-to-air missiles; two AIM-9M short range air-to-air missiles and four AIM-120D AMRAAM radar guided medium range missiles, suspended from pylons beneath the sleek raptor-like wings. McQuade shrugged on his G-suit and clambered up the ladder as maintenance officers swarmed over him. His breathing was ragged; his blood fizzing with surging adrenalin. Despite his training, his heart was racing and his hands felt clammy. Inside the big hollow hangar the sounds of frantic activity seemed to echo.

Other maintenance crew were crawling beneath the wings of the Viper, pulling safety pins from missiles, pushing closed access panels and removing wheel chocks, each of them moving with the coordinated unflustered efficiency that comes from discipline and repetition.

McQuade pulled on his new helmet while one of the enlisted crew chiefs clipped his harness to the parachute risers of the ejection seat and fastened his safety belt. McQuade flipped the battery and JFS switches. Around him the Viper suddenly began to come alive. Cockpit lights flickered, needles on the instrument display began to move, and the huge engine started to growl.

McQuade could hear the blood singing in his ears. He stole a glance sideways and made eye contact with Hernandez.

McQuade wondered whether the other pilot could sense his nervous exhilaration. His radio crackled to life in his ears.

"Gunslinger, check Victor." The two pilots would be known as Gunslinger One and Two for the mission.

"Two!" McQuade responded immediately on VHF.

"Gunslinger check," Hernandez said again, this time repeating the instruction on his fighter's main UHF radio.

"Two!"

Hernandez caught the attention of his crew chief standing in front of his Viper by quickly flicking the taxi light on and off then twirled his finger to indicate he was ready to taxi from the hangar. The crew chief marshaled the Viper forward then gave the all-clear and saluted. Hernandez eased the throttle ahead with his left hand and the Viper began to roll towards the open hangar doors and the daylight beyond. McQuade followed ten seconds later, and the two fighters met on alternating sides of the taxiway.

*

The Vipers climbed to twenty thousand feet and raced east in tactical formation, line abreast, with nearly two miles of sky separating them. McQuade leaned forward against his shoulder straps and scanned the sky. Tight apprehension, like a delicious kind of dread, slithered in his guts.

The Supervisor of Flying (SOF) at Lutsk Air Base directed the pilots to contact an AWACS circling high over western Ukraine. Hernandez reached for his up-front control and programmed in the AWACS strike frequency.

"Chariot. Gunslinger One."

"Gunslinger. Chariot has you five by five," the controller aboard the modified Boeing 707-320B replied. "Authenticate Foxtrot November."

Among the pilot's reference paperwork in the cockpit was a small booklet containing classified codes that were used to authenticate radio communications to ensure the validity of each party. Hernandez thumbed through the book and drew his finger along the matrix until he found the reply for 'FN'

"Chariot. Gunslinger One authenticates Whiskey Alfa."

The controller's tone aboard the AWACS seemed to relax a little. He passed on target details quickly.

"Gunslinger One, Chariot. Bogeys are twelve plus Tango Uniform niner five bombers, bullseye two-seven-one for three sixty, two-three thousand, east."

"Gunslinger One, copy," responded Hernandez.

With the Bear bombers still more than three hundred miles away, the F-16's radar was not powerful enough to begin the process of tracking the Russian aircraft. Hernandez's eyes flicked between the Viper's HUD display, raw gear, and the radar scope in a rhythmic cross check of all his available data. He dropped the Viper's engine power back to eighty percent to conserve fuel and a few seconds later McQuade mirrored the maneuver, easing his throttle out of afterburner. Hernandez re-contacted the AWACS for a Sit Rep.

The controller disregarded typical comms brevity and gave the pilot a succinct brief. "Ukrainian partisans and infantry regulars on the outskirts of the capital have come under heavy Russian bombing attack. Command thinks it's a prelude to an armored assault. The Ukrainians contacted Theater Command for urgent help."

"Roger, Chariot."

The two F-16s made the minor course correction onto their new heading and flew on, racing towards the skies over Kiev at three hundred and fifty miles an hour. As the minutes to intercept ticked down, McQuade felt the tension ratchet up. Visibility was obscured by a thick haze of smoke drifting up from the bomb-ravaged city that lay on the far horizon. He set the range of his radar to forty-mile scope with a search altitude of twenty thousand feet and above then adjusted the volume on his radar threat warning receiver. In his mind he began to visualize the intercept, imagining the hapless Russian bombers as the two Vipers pounced on them.

The Tu-95 'Bear' was a large, lumbering four-engine turboprop powered strategic bomber that had been in active service since the 1950s. It was the size of a passenger airliner and had a top speed of around four hundred miles an hour. If the Russian bombers were still over Kiev when the Vipers pounced, they would be defenseless prey.

McQuade scanned the skies and dared to hope. An unprotected enemy bomber was every fighter pilot's dream target. The Vipers closed to within one hundred nautical miles of Kiev and McQuade leaned forward to fiddle with his radar instruments to make certain it was patched into the feed from the AWACS. His scope began displaying raw hits.

Suddenly the voice of the circling AWACS controller was loud in both pilots ears, the sound crackling and hissing with static.

"Gunslinger One. Chariot. Bears over Kiev bugging out east. New threat! Bogeys bullseye one-three-six! Four-ship single group, zero-zero-five, one-zero-zero nautical miles, one-two thousand. Commit! Commit!" the message came over the secure radio channel.

In a heartbeat the tactical situation for the Vipers had changed from a classic single side off-set intercept on a formation of lumbering bombers to facing an unknown enemy fighter threat – and they were outnumbered four to two.

Instinctively Hernandez and McQuade flicked their eyes to the north, peering out through their bubble canopies towards the approaching threat, just one hundred miles away and closing on them fast.

Hernandez's voice had an edge of apprehension and urgency to it when he replied. "Roger, Chariot. Gunslinger One!"

*

"Gunslinger, Chariot…" The AWACS operator's voice came loudly through both pilots' helmet comms. Hernandez and McQuade had turned and were racing towards the approaching bogeys. "Contacts Bogey now zero-zero-seven, nine-zero nautical miles, one-four thousand. Possible two-groups."

"Gunslinger, copy," Hernandez acknowledged. His Viper's instrumentation was downloading the feed from the AWACS aircraft, and he kept an eye on the display between scanning the blue sky around him for contrails.

As the American fighters converged on the threat, McQuade made his preparations, flipping switches in the cockpit to activate his fire-control systems and turning the Master Arm switch 'on'. He scanned the weapons status display which blinked back at him with a row of green lights.

Hernandez's voice was tense in his helmet comms.

"Gunslinger Two, arm 'em up."

The voice of the young controller on the E-3 interrupted the routine checks.

"Gunslinger, Bogeys now zero-zero-seven, eight-zero nautical miles, one-five thousand. Request VID."

"Copy, Chariot. Bogey type?" Hernandez asked, looking for any information on why the approaching aircraft had not yet been declared hostile.

"Gunslinger, reported MiG two-nine Fulcrums."

The news made Hernandez's eyebrows furrow in consternation if not surprise.

The Mikoyan MiG-29 'Fulcrum' was a twin-engine fighter designed during the Soviet Cold War era to counter the then-new American F-15 Eagle and the F-16. The MiG had been in active operation since the early 1980s and had proven itself a formidable fighter in conflicts around the world.

Hernandez dwelt on the tactical situation for a moment, and grudgingly conceded that the Russians who had planned the Tu-95 bombing mission on the outskirts of Kiev had been crafty, cunning bastards. They had attacked the city with the long-range bombers and then used them to bait American interceptors. It had been neatly done. The idea of picking off a swathe of slow lumbering bombers was a lot more appealing to

Hernandez than going head-to-head against a superior number of high-quality fighters.

The bandits closed within seventy nautical miles. The two Vipers were flying at twenty-three thousand feet, still well above the approaching targets and maintaining their height advantage.

Hernandez tried to put himself in the cockpit of the lead bandit. They would be flying an intercept course to cover the retreat of their bombers, still unaware of his exact location, but no doubt expecting American fighters to have launched in pursuit. Had they anticipated that two F-16s would have scrambled immediately, or would the enemy fighters expect the Americans to fly head-on into the trap they were preparing to spring?

He made a decision. *Standard off-set. Visual intercept. No lock.*

"Gunslinger, Lead, come left two-five-zero. Snooze the radars," he ordered.

"Two."

The two Vipers began banking left.

Hernandez checked his threat receiver and confirmed the Vipers remained undetected. He turned his head, peering around the heads-up display (HUD) at the front of his canopy. The bandits were passing by, fifty nautical miles to the north. Hernandez held his course for sixty more tense seconds and then brought the two Vipers around, aggressively pointing the nose of his jet towards the threat until they were west of the enemy aircraft but quickly closing in, still undetected, and still maintaining their precious height advantage.

The Vipers closed on the unsuspecting bandits quickly. The F-16s were on the offensive. McQuade's keen eyes spotted the distant pale specks first and he raised the alert. Hernandez narrowed his gaze, checking for reflections of sunlight. He caught a glint of bright light off a cockpit canopy allowing his eyes to focus. The Russians were flying in a pair of two-ship formations, about twenty miles ahead but just beginning a gentle turn towards the south. The Vipers were within missile range – but remained 'weapons-hold', waiting until they got

VID. Hernandez took an instant to study the configuration of the bogeys as the space between the hunters and the hunted closed. They were twin-rudder fighters, painted light grey against the cobalt blue of the sky. At a distance they looked like F-15s. He waited until he was absolutely certain.

"Chariot, Gunslinger One. Confirm. VIDs are four ship MiG two-nine Fulcrums east bound. Bandits! Bandits! Bandits! Confirm cleared to engage!" Hernandez informed the AWACS as he switched his weapons selector from his medium range AMRAAM missiles to his heat-seeking AIM-9Ms.

"Roger, Gunslinger One," the controller verified as the cockpit of Hernandez's Viper filled with the warbling sound of his missiles beginning to acquire a tone. "Confirm hostile. Cleared to engage."

Hernandez took a last long settling breath. "Gunslinger Two, target trail group," he said. Then, more solemnly, to give the moment its due significance, he added, "Vipers, let's go to war."

McQuade uncaged the AIM-9M Sidewinder slung beneath the fighter's left wingtip and heard the distinct growl of the weapon's IR seeker almost immediately. The tone in his headset changed suddenly to a high-pitched screech as the TD centered on his target. The missile was growling its anxiety, it had sensed the enemy fighter's jet blasts and already it was tracking, howling its eagerness to kill. A cold savage blade of vengeful hatred burned within McQuade as he unleashed the missile and watched the bright flash of its launch. "Gunslinger Two. Fox Two!" McQuade declared over their inter-flight VHF frequency, his voice strangled and rough.

"Gunslinger One. Fox Two!" Hernandez said a split-second later.

The two AIM-9Ms leapt off their rails like darts, corkscrewing and skidding away across the sky towards the formation of trailing MiG fighters, the short-range heat-seeking missiles hunting like bloodhounds.

McQuade's Sidewinder swerved unerringly towards the nearest enemy fighter. At the very last moment the Russian pilot saw death approaching. He had only just begun to turn away from the danger when the missile tore off the MiG's starboard wing.

The shock wave of the sudden violent explosion washed over the Viper. The Fulcrum disintegrated in the sky. The severed wing went cartwheeling across the clouds and the fighter became enveloped in a bright bloom of fire and smoke. Within a matter of seconds, both of the trailing Russian jets had erupted into fireballs, tumbling out of the air as blazing mangled wreckage.

The two surviving Mig-29 Fulcrums split apart into a panic of chaotic dives and climbs, each pilot frantically trying to put lift vectors and Gs towards the incoming danger. The enemy jets went to full power and turned tightly into the diving Vipers that trailed them, pumping out flares to turn the sky into a chaos of smoke and confusion.

Hernandez set his sights on the left hand MiG-29 of the lead formation. He armed his last remaining AIM-9M and lined up the target designator TD box on his HUD with the target. He pickled the launch button and the F-16 rocked and swayed as the missile ignited.

"Fox Two!"

The Vipers accelerated for the merge. McQuade got a faint hum of tone in his headphones, indicating his remaining AIM-9M Sidewinder had picked up the scent of another Russian warplane's engine. He fired impulsively.

"Gunslinger Two. Fox Two!"

At the same moment the MiG-29 converging towards him fired a missile. The weapons passed each other in the air and then the Russian pilot fired off flares. The sky became filled with bright light, vapor trails, and howling engines.

McQuade's launched Sidewinder veered away from its target, drawn to the bright glowing lure of the Russian flares and detonated harmlessly in a bloom of black smoke. But the enemy missiles continued to close unerringly on the Viper.

McQuade threw his fighter into a hard 9-G turn, twisting his aircraft as the Russian air-to-air missile stalked him. He toggled off another string of flares and then suddenly cut power and jinked right. The Russian missile flew past harmlessly, missing the American fighter's wing by fifty feet.

The Mig-29s were nimble, agile adversaries, but they were carrying limited fuel. One of the surviving Russian pilots put his plane's nose down steeply and made a desperate dive for the ground.

McQuade saw the MiG attempting to flee. He turned and dived in pursuit. The F-16C had a speed advantage. McQuade's fighter closed remorselessly. He selected two of the AMRAAM missiles hanging beneath his wings.

"Fox Three!" McQuade called the shots.

The AMRAAMS were sophisticated missiles that incorporated a datalink or ships radar to guide the weapon to a point where its active radar turned on and began a terminal intercept of the target. The 'fire-and-forget' feature freed the Viper pilots to seek out fresh targets almost immediately, allowing for instant switches between weapons.

The Russian pilot seemed to slow in the sky as if he sensed his inevitable demise. He was at three thousand feet when the AMRAAMs struck the starboard wing, cleaving it clean off the aircraft's fuselage. The MiG went spiraling wildly into the ground and exploded in a huge eruption of flames and oily smoke.

The remaining MiG had the opportunity to flee; the F-16 Vipers were low on missiles, and both sides were low on fuel. But the Russian pilot instead fell vengefully from the high clouds and locked onto the tail of McQuade's Viper. McQuade heard his threat warning indicator loud in his ears. He jinked left intuitively, and then turned hard to the right, his proximity to the ground below restricting his ability to take evasive measures. The Russian pilot fired a short range infrared-homing air-to-air missile. McQuade filled the sky around him with chaff and flares and then pulled into the vertical and banked right. At the top of his climb he made a tight aerobatic turn and plunged into a dive. The Russian pilot saw McQuade's Viper begin to climb and anticipated the

American's maneuver. As soon as McQuade began to turn over at the apex of his climb, the MiG went into a climb of its own, arrowing towards the sun. McQuade followed, going vertical, but the Viper lacked the energy to overhaul the Fulcrum. Then the Russian pilot turned out unexpectedly, presenting McQuade with his six-o'clock.

The Russian pilot began a tight turn and McQuade stayed on target, keeping the enemy fighter within the display of his HUD, but still too far away to fire guns. Sensing imminent danger, the Russian pilot threw his aircraft around the sky, trying to gain energy and hoping to force the American on his tail into an overshoot. McQuade wrestled with the Viper's controls as the nimble MiG swayed elusively in and out of his sights.

The Viper was traveling too fast; it shot past the Fulcrum as the Russian pilot hauled his fighter into a sudden tight turn. The Viper had too much energy to match the bank – it flashed across the sky, suddenly defensive as the Russian aircraft hooked around onto its tail.

McQuade could feel himself sweating inside his flight suit. The sound of his ragged breathing was loud in his own ears. His threat warning indicator broke out into strident, warbling warning. He flung the Viper into a roll, bleeding off speed, twisting left and right to scrub off energy. The MiG-29 arrowed past the Viper as McQuade made another desperate jink – the Russian fighter's fuselage reflecting sunlight and its sleek swept-back wings glinting evil intent as it flashed across the Viper's nose.

McQuade seized his opportunity, turning to keep the MiG in the sights of his HUD as the distance between the two aircraft stabilized. The sensitive pipper on his HUD wavered and then came to rest on the canopy of the MiG. He thumbed the trigger on his joystick and the M61A1 Vulcan 6-barrel 20mm cannon roared into life.

McQuade watched the streak of bullets arc out across the void, merging with the enemy fighter in a sudden explosive fireball of smoke and flame.

*

Hernandez sat drenched in sweat, wrung out with fatigue and exhaustion. He flicked his eyes over his fuel status readout, his mind still numb and oversaturated with the intense fear and adrenalin of air combat. McQuade's Viper was off his left wing, the fighters flying west at nineteen thousand feet. Hernandez's fingers inside his gloves were cold and trembling uncontrollably. It was the first time he had ever been involved in air-to-air combat; the chaos and terror and savagery of the experience had left him profoundly shaken.

McQuade too sat in his cockpit panting, his breath rasping across his throat. There was a feeling of triumphant retribution, like a clenched fist, knotted in his chest. In his mind he replayed the moment the MiG in his sights suddenly exploded under the hammering chatter of his cannon.

That was for Maksim, he thought vengefully.

The Vipers flashed over the outskirts of Kiev and the gray desolation of entire suburbs flattened to rubble so that even the roads had been obliterated by wreckage. Fires and smoke rose from the smoldering ruins. In between the bomb-devastated carnage were scattered small untouched patches of green grass, not yet ploughed under by the churning steel tracks of Russian tanks. The landscape seemed parched and austere.

They turned a few degrees north and boomed over a chain of small reservoirs, the water so dark blue as to appear almost black at altitude. Ugly grey factory blocks arranged in ranks slid beneath their wingtips. Further north the entire horizon was obscured by a filthy brown skirt of smoke and dust; the ominous telltale trail of the main Russian Army advancing.

A crackle of static and then an urgent voice in their headsets broke the sense of gloomy foreboding.

"All players! All Players! This is Chariot calling for emergency close air support…"

Hernandez heard the open frequency call and involuntarily flinched. McQuade reacted like a man punched hard in the guts. He heard himself gasp, and a cold clammy sense of dread washed over him. His eyes snapped to his fuel status. He was close to 'Joker'.

Hernandez dutifully responded to the call.

"Chariot. Gunslinger flight, checking in. We are a two-ship by Fox One Six ten nautical miles north of Kiev, flight level one-nine zero, almost Winchester 20mm rounds and carrying AMRAAMs. We have just six minutes of playtime before bingo fuel. Other options? Over."

"Negative, Gunslinger flight. No other responders," Chariot said abruptly. "Stand by for AO update."

Ukrainian regular troops and a group of partisans defending buildings in the west of Kiev were under heavy attack from Russian APCs and a Su-25 'Frogfoot' ground-attack jet fighter. McQuade felt a sick slide of déjà vu tie a knot in his guts.

"Location, Chariot?"

"JTAC call sign Weasel," the controller said, then passed along the grid reference.

McQuade reeled with the shock of recognition. He switched his radio to the inter-flight VHF frequency.

"One, I know the location. I have friends down there."

"Rog," Hernandez replied. He paused for a long moment and then reconnected with the AWACS controller who had made the 'all players' call.

"Gunslinger flight commits."

"Gunslinger push VHF Red one four. Red one four asap. Troops in combat."

The two Vipers turned to the south east and began to sink down the sky. Hernandez keyed his mike.

"Weasel. Weasel, this is Gunslinger flight; we are two Fox One Six responding. Over."

Gunslinger, Weasel, AO update. I'm a JTAC embedded with a Ukraine infantry company and one hundred plus partisans in buildings surrounding 'The Shrine to Heroes of Ukraine'. We've got a strong Russian force of PCs marshaling to the north of our position preparing to attack. Multiple

MANPADS in the area and we are under air-to-ground attack from a single enemy Sierra Uniform two five. Say when ready nine-line."

"Ready nine-line," Hernandez replied immediately.

The JTAC gave the details of their exact location, grid references and the target types. Hernandez repeated.

"Good read back," the JTAC on the ground had a thick Ukraine accent, his voice seeming to come in waves through the hiss of static and a background of automatic weapons fire.

Hernandez and McQuade turned further south and dived.

McQuade spotted it first; a pencil line of black smoke rising into the air above a rectangle of bleak grey government blocks. The buildings were arranged around a vast paved quadrangle of open space, and in the center was a raised platform, like a low stage. McQuade felt a wave of emotions washed over him. He cast his eyes towards the highest, southernmost building and gave an audible gasp. The tiny waving patch of blue and yellow fabric hanging from the top of the flagpole made a brave, defiant splash of color against the bleak grey sky. The fabric was stained and frayed and bullet holed – but McQuade felt a choke of emotion. He lost count how many brave Ukrainian partisans had given their lives to protect that precious piece of fabric and all that it symbolized.

The two Vipers increased speed and went onto the attack. Their priority was to eliminate the air threat. Only once that task was accomplished would they make use of the nine-line report to confront the Russian ground threat.

Near the buildings along the western edge of the quadrangle McQuade saw something glint briefly against the dull grey background, and he narrowed his eyes and peered more carefully until he could make out the shape of something weaving and swerving above the ground, its pattern of painted camouflage diffusing its lethal shape.

"Su-25," McQuade said. "Starboard of the western buildings. It's turning to make another ground-attack."

"Rog," Hernandez said. They were rushing down the sky so swiftly that second-by-second the details of the drama being played out on the battlefield filled quickly.

The Ukrainian infantry and partisans occupied the eastern, northern and western buildings surrounding the 'The Shrine to Heroes of Ukraine' and were being pressed on all sides by advancing Russian infantry. To the north, enemy APCs were marshaling for a wave of support attacks, while overhead the Su-25 strafed the closest buildings, bringing death from the air.

One of the northern buildings was on fire. The smoke boiled black and rose straight into the windless air. Lying in drifts across the road and around each of the apartment buildings were the bodies of dead soldiers. They had been flung down carelessly, their shapes twisted, piled upon each other in places. The gruesome sight stirred McQuade. A feeling of deep resentment overwhelmed him until he could taste the bitter hatred in his throat.

From darkened windows of the bullet-ravaged buildings McQuade could see flashing winks of light where the Ukrainians still fought on. Some of the soldiers were firing at the Su-25 with small arms as the ungainly, gruesome bird of prey turned and circled back for another attack.

The Frogfoot made a wide, lazy sweep across the sky and leveled its wings, settling a few hundred feet above the ground as it swooped on its next strafing run. The Russian pilot had his eyes fixed on a second-story row of windows in the northern façade of the nearest building.

"One is in!" Hernandez declared and lined his Viper up for a pass, yawing sideways in the sky until he hung directly behind the Russian jet's tail, while McQuade climbed and circled to cover Hernandez's six o'clock and to line himself up for a high-angle support attack if the Su-25 survived.

The Frogfoot opened fire on the building, and the aircraft's 30mm GSh-2-30 dual-barrel autocannon roared. The Su-25 was the Russian version of the lethal American A-10 Warthog. The cannon spat flickering tongues of fire as it blazed, gouging concrete chunks from the wall and disintegrating windows with a sound like a thundering jackhammer.

McQuade watched the horror, leaning his head against the canopy of his fighter to witness the terrible carnage. "Die, you bastard! Die!" he whispered as he leveled his fighter out two miles behind Hernandez and a hundred feet higher. He felt a sudden stab of propriety – as though the brave Ukrainians enduring the terrible tempest were his kin, and a cold callous outrage came over him. He selected the Viper's cannon on his weapons display and saw he had less than two hundred rounds of ammunition remaining.

Ahead and below him, Hernandez had launched his swooping attack on the Russian jet, overhauling the slower, ungainly Su-25 and then suddenly opening fire. But at the same instant the Viper's tracer bullets streamed from the cannon, the Russian Frogfoot wobbled its wings, seemed to stall in the air, and then dropped fifty feet towards the ground. The sudden full-flap maneuver caught Hernandez by surprise. He was already committed to his angle of attack, his speed too high to respond to the Russian's ploy. The stream of tracer bullets roared from the Viper, flying high and wide. Then the F-16 was climbing steeply, pumping out flares and chaff to fend off Russian infantry shoulder-mounted SAMS as Hernandez clawed at the sky for altitude and raged his frustration.

McQuade reacted instinctively, angling the Viper's nose down and diving to intercept the Russian. The Su-25 was turning to port, tilted on one wing as it hugged the ground. McQuade cut across the Frogfoot's path and eased back power to slow himself down through the air. Gradually, inexorably, the Russian ground-attack jet continued its turn, seeming to McQuade to be moving in slow motion. He jinked the nose of the fighter a couple of times and then saw the Russian jet fly straight across his sights. The enemy plane was angled into its lumbering turn so that McQuade could see the pilot through the clear Perspex of his canopy. His helmet was bright blue, his face lifted up to McQuade's – and although the man's features were hidden behind face mask and visor, McQuade sensed the other pilot's helpless fatalistic acceptance.

Good! McQuade thought coldly. *I want you to know you're about to die, you murdering Russian bastard!*

McQuade's finger curled around the trigger. He waited a heartbeat longer. The Russian was not even maneuvering to avoid the Viper's attack. Out of the corner of his eye, to the north, McQuade could see hundreds of Russian soldiers dismounting from BMP-2 troop carriers.

"Altitude! Altitude!" Bitchin' Betty's automatic voice began to chant in McQuade's headset. The sound seemed to galvanize and focus him into action. He squeezed the trigger and the Viper's cannon roared.

He was on target for just three seconds, and then the Su-25 had flown past as McQuade continued his line of flight, climbing for altitude and twisting around him in the tight confines of his ejection seat to look back over his shoulder and judge the impact of his attack.

The Russian plane was still flying and McQuade felt an instant of utter dismay. He had seen his bullets converge on the target. He had seen the enemy plane shudder violently in the air as the 20mm rounds tore through the fuselage.

He put the Viper into a near vertical climb, pushing the throttle forward. His RWR scope was filled with a clutter of warnings which he ignored. He toggled off chaff and a string of flares, then looked once more back over his shoulder.

The Su-25 was gliding slowly through the air, its wings level but gradually sinking down the sky. McQuade watched, fascinated. The Su-25's shadow across the ground rose up quickly to meet the belly of the stricken plane. Then the Frogfoot crashed into a nearby forest and exploded in a vast fireball of flames and smoke, flattening a stand of trees and gouging a black oil-streaked crater in the earth.

McQuade punched the air and let out a savage growl of triumph. Now his priority was to gain altitude and clear the area. He was perilously low on fuel; his warning display on the

HUD flashed a blinking alert, and the automated voice of 'Bitchin' Betty' cried, "Bingo fuel! Bingo fuel!"

But he wanted to make one last defiant gesture of solidarity with the Ukrainian freedom fighters down on the battlefield. He threw the Viper over and then put the aircraft into a tight turn, the big jet engine roaring as he swung to the south and sank lower and lower.

When he was just a few hundred feet above the ground, he flashed over the flag that still hung defiant from 'The Shrine to Heroes of Ukraine' flagpole, rocking his wings from side to side in tribute and celebration.

As he streaked past, he could see Ukraine soldiers leaning out from the windows of the surrounding buildings, cheering him.

He turned for Lutsk and began to climb once again, then poignantly remembered the many heroic rebels who had fought and died delivering that flag to the shrine. Maksim's words echoed in his ears, so clear that it seemed as if the Ukrainian freedom fighter was sitting in the cockpit beside him.

"For as long as the Ukraine flag flies over the Shrine to Heroes, the fight for freedom will go on. The flag is a tribute to the generations of patriots who made this country great; a symbol of solidarity and faith eternal. Whilst ever the flag flies in defiance of our oppressors, Ukraine has hope."

Facebook: https://www.facebook.com/NickRyanWW3
Website: https://www.worldwar3timeline.com

Author's Note:

The city of Kiev has several magnificent and historical landmarks, some of which date back many hundreds of years. Unfortunately the *Svyatynya heroyam Ukrayiny* 'Shrine to Heroes of Ukraine', only exists in my imagination. I hope readers will forgive my small fiction for the sake of the story.

Acknowledgements:

The greatest thrill of writing, for me, is the opportunity to research the subject matter and to work with military, political and historical experts from around the world. I had a lot of help researching this book from the following people. I am forever grateful for their willing enthusiasm and cooperation.

Any remaining technical errors are mine and were the result of deliberate choices I made for the sake of the narrative.

Randall Haskin:

Randall is a retired USAF pilot who served in the US Air Force for over twenty years as a fighter pilot and instructor. He is now a commercial airline pilot. Randall helped me with all the intricate F-16 sequences in the novel, guiding me through each scene to help me clearly understand the terminology, the technology and the communication procedures between pilots to ensure I had a clear grasp of the details.

Jill Blasy:

Jill has the editorial eye of an eagle! I trust Jill to read every manuscript, picking up typographical errors, missing commas, and for her general 'sense' of the book. Jill has been a great friend and a valuable part of my team for several years.

Jan Wade:

Jan is my Personal Assistant and an indispensable part of my team. She is a thoughtful, thorough, professional and persistent pleasure to work with. Chances are, if you're reading this book, it's due to Jan's engaging marketing and promotional efforts.

Scott 'Hurler' Weaver:

Scott is a retired Lt. Colonel with the USAF and presently works as a pilot with American Airlines. Scott is also the author of *'Pilots of Thunderbird Field'* and *'A Pilot's Passion: Baseball Travels the World'*.

https://www.scottrweaver.com

As a senior pilot, Scott has over 2,600 hours of instructor and fighter time. He flew as an F-16C fighter pilot at Hahn Air Base, West Germany, as well as the DC ANG at Andrews AFB, Maryland.

Scott was a constant source of information throughout the writing process, ensuring the combat sequences were as authentic as possible, and providing countless small details of information that contributed to the book's realism.

Scott checked over every F-16 scene in the book, and was a heartening source of encouragement and inspiration throughout the writing process.

Printed in Great Britain
by Amazon